Mongolian Horse

Mongolian Horse

Stories

David E. Yee

www.blacklawrence.com

Executive Editor: Diane Goettel
Cover Design: Kalynn Burke
Book Design: Amy Freels

Published 2022 by Black Lawrence Press.
Printed in the United States.

Contents

For Sara, for Katie, for Gerris, for Beth.

Heaven for Your Full Lungs

When I surface, I fold my blazer over the edge of the tank, rip the left sleeve off my dress shirt, and use it to tie the mass of my hair behind my head. The shoulder of the linen had been torn in my fall, so I don't mind ruining the garment, but I shouldn't have forgotten my hair ties, not for a formal gig. This is after I've coughed the night-thick water from my stomach, that final heave like vomiting. Then I sink, forearms holding me to the lip of the glass walls that form a square around me, ten by ten, transparent but sturdy, like the bulletproof slabs bank tellers work behind. For a moment, I can recall the sensation of being in a pool early in the season, how you have to descend into the water for warmth. I blink my eyelashes dry, and by this time Benji has heaved out his minestrone in the tank adjacent to mine. I stand and say, "Tell me I'm pretty." And he chuckles, "Tell me I'm fun."

I climb free of my death and join the others doing the same. Balancing on the edge of the glass as I climb over it, I can see the other vessels—identical to mine except for their contents—stretching out and blurring together in the distance. Before I jump down into the narrow channel of white tile that forms a grid between the tanks, I remember those nights when, as a teenager, I'd sneak out over the backyard fence toward Jerome's warehouse apartment. I'd learned to play the drums while he figured out his off-brand Telecaster. That memory is so far away now—a song I know half the words to.

I take Benji's hand, gripping his armpit to help him over. He says, "Thanks, Thump," as he brushes chunks of pasta and carrot from his tank top and boxers. He died in the Bolton Hill apartment he used to share with his cousin, had a coronary event while eating soup, fell face-first into it, paralyzed. He'll always be forty-one. He said once, while he rubbed the thin spot on his scalp, "At least I shaved that day. Can you imagine, an eternity of stubble?" We go to my catty-corner neighbor, Roberta, and ease her over, the wet ends of her hair threading the wrinkles on her back. She'd slipped as she settled into the tub at her old folks' home, has a jagged scar on her temple and a bruise in the shape of a rose on her lower back. Benji cleans himself in her tepid bathwater, lapping it over the glass and onto his limbs.

Usually, Benji and I walk together. Some days we split up. Occasionally, I stay in and list on my back in the water, dark as the sky I drowned under. My first waking, while I was thrashing around, Benji came to the edge of my tank. He said, "It's okay. You're okay now." I must have looked like a swamp creature, the black coils of my hair cascading wet across my face. I was still calling for help. Benji asked where I'd been. My nostrils burned, my throat raw from the coughing. I'd been on a boat—no, a yacht—with strings of lights suspended between lattices on the bow. I remember looking up at them while I played, charmed by the way their yellow glow made the chrome on my drum kit shine, the stripes in the maple darkening in contrast. Jerome had just finished some banter with the audience, and we started "Beast of Burden." It was Jerome's idea—playing for a wedding band, earning steadier money—and I went along because I could barely make rent, and it beat waiting tables on the weekend.

After the set, I got too drunk and fell overboard. I don't know how long I was treading water, shouting, "Wait!" until my throat ached. The chill of the sea wind caught me in the back of the mouth. Twenty feet off, the boat, swollen with light, bobbed with the current. I'd considered myself a capable swimmer, but after ten strokes, I knew I couldn't match its pace. When I tried to float, panic made my breath unsteady. On the deck, the music had been so loud the cones in the speakers popped with the kick, but from the water, I couldn't tell the tempo of the song, slurred by the distance. It was hard, wanting the hands of the world to catch me, to slow the ship, to pull my body from the Chesapeake and return it to the party. When the yacht was just a spec, a murmur on the horizon, I was alone with the water. As I kicked off my Oxfords to shed some weight, I knew there was nothing watching over me.

That first time, Benji listened to a less concise retelling, nodding as I described the feeling of slipping under, of reaching above my head and feeling only more of the Bay, the bitter taste of the murky water as it eased past my tongue. Then, the terror of surrender. He'd said, "Well it's all over. I'm Benji." Running my fingers over the surface, I was confused by the cube of the Chesapeake that encased me. I reached out to shake his hand, said, "My name is Theodore. Everybody calls me Thump."

He'd been right—though I was soaked from my scalp to the soles of my feet, I felt calm, restful even. There are no burdens for the dead. Is there a need to fret about what you can't remedy? Today, like that first day, we greet the people drowned around us in our—for lack of a better term—neighborhood. The language of life falls short here. There are no *days*. We talk and explore until we wake, again, in the liquid that carried us here. It happens in a moment. Trying to recall something specific, like the smell of your apartment, the tone of the air as cars whip past on the cross street, and when the memory falls away in a laugh at the end of an anecdote, or the eyes-closed exhale punctuating a private thought, there is a lapse, a lightheadedness—a release and submersion— then the sudden desire to breathe.

∾

I fold my blazer on the edge of the tank, rip off my sleeve, tie the mass of my hair behind my head. Every single time, I hate the briny taste of the Chesapeake as I purge it past my throat. Lowering myself in the water to my chin, I wait for the shivering in my flanks to ease, and when I can see again, Benji is smiling. I rise and say, "Tell me I'm pretty."

"Tell me I'm fun."

I help him over, then we free Roberta, and she says, "Such lovely gentlemen, you are." Her skin smells like lavender soap, the kind my mother kept in the half bathroom growing up.

No one understands how long each cycle lasts. The order of our cells is untraceable. We don't busy ourselves with figuring it out. Instead, we climb into the channels and converse like actors after a show, discussing our lives as if they were a performance. For every suicide, there is an accident. For every murder victim, a failed rescue. Someone told me once that stories, here, aren't just currency, they're our blood, our breath. It is entirely possible to avoid change—to gather your former wants, wishes, and regrets into one neglected place in your mind and spend your time socializing with the dead around you. But when you share something personal here, people listen, and there is motion to that, a slow kind of unburdening.

Benji says, "You know, a lot of musicians end up drowning. I have a theory—what makes a musician if not a love of rhythm? Every instrument is some kind of vibration. My cousin used to play this clarinet with a messed-up mouthpiece. Her reed just buzzed and buzzed. Drove me crazy. But anyways, every musician I've ever met, all the real ones, they can't get away from rhythm. Always tapping their feet or bobbing their heads. They need a pulse, and water has one. I mean, it's never *really* still, right?" He holds his hand between us, swaying. "Maybe it draws you guys in. You know Art, the saxophonist? He's around here somewhere. He'll back me up on this."

Today I lead our walk, turning left past cells of miniature lakes, pool water fuming chlorine, so many oceans lapping at the lips of their containers. A woman with mud in her dress reaches over into a lukewarm bath, submerges herself like she's bobbing for apples and comes up with a baby, pale bottom held in the crook of her arm. Benji touches the crown of its head as it cries the fluid from its lungs. He says, "Hi Jessica." She says hello, patting the child on the back. Then the baby is serene, smiling with a finger in its mouth, and Jessica says, "There, there."

Conversations about drowning, about death, always turn personal. I don't usually offer the more precise details of that night, but this doesn't stop Benji from asking about them. Benji says, "Were you a drinker? I mean, did you always get drunk at gigs?" I told him sure, the guys and I used to get after it, but this was rowdier than usual because I'd gotten into a fight with my girlfriend, Andy. Benji stops a moment, looking at me like he's noticing, for the first time, the color of my eyes. He says, "She's always the first thing you bring up. Did you love her?" And he's so close to shaking with passion as he asks that I can't help laughing. He says, "Don't be like that, it's a serious question."

I say, "It's hard to recall. I spent a lot of time wondering what she saw in me." She was sharp in a way that made me uncomfortable and yet excited to talk to her. God, the way her face bent when she laughed at me. That posh haircut, her olive skin. "You know, she used to call me Chop Stick? She's the only one I'd ever let get away with that." After a while, my clothes dry out.

Benji puts his hand on my shoulder. "What'd you fight about?"

We turn and turn again, stepping slowly across the damp tile. There is no reason to remember your way back. I say, "It feels weird now how much we made out of nothing." Jerome had booked that Rock-the-Boat gig on the Bay. It paid shit, but he negotiated a plus-one for everyone in the band—we figured we'd just party. I'd been with Andy for three years by then, but Jerome had barely settled down, was still jittery about everything being *just so*. He got annoyed I had my hair down, but my hair ties were back in the car, and we'd already set out. I figured he'd get over it. Andy and I snuck off after the second set. I say, "She used to lead me by the hand to those off-limits places. She was confident like that. I'd never go by myself."

Benji pauses at a crossing, saying, "Maybe you would've. You were young."

"We went through the kitchen to this backroom where they kept seating for the deck. I could taste the merlot on her lips, could see the tint of it on her front teeth. She sat on a table, brought me to her. I wish I could've gone then. Just dropped dead. That would make for a nice afterlife."

Benji laughs. "I don't think it works quite like that."

$\sim$

Sometimes I check my pockets for a misplaced hair tie nestled in a divot of cloth. My pants and jackets used to be full of them. I fold my blazer, rip off my sleeve. Steve, my neighbor on the other side, is a child, says, "Gosh," as he blows the green mud from his nose into his creek water layered with dead leaves. Then he jumps free and takes off running. Benji and I have spent a few days walking in different directions. I smile to him. "Tell me I'm pretty."

"Tell me I'm fun."

Roberta says, "Thank you gentlemen."

We join a group of men and women using their arms to spin the Johnson & Johnson-bubbled water of a tub nearby, swirling an infant from the middle and into the hands of a man named Bon whose hairy chest has flecks of puke in it. Benji waves, and Bon uses the baby's hand to wave back.

"We need to find a guy named Wilhelm," Benji says. "Everyone keeps talking about how he passed in a kiddie pool filled with champagne." I ask him if he liked the taste of it enough to search it out. He says, "In life? No, not really. I never was a drinker. I guess that's why I didn't get invited out much. Or maybe it was the other way around." The skin on his forehead goes taut as his brows pinch shadows around his eyes. He says, "Who's to say now?"

We start down a channel of Indonesian families reuniting—men and women pulling their children, their neighbors from the cloudy water, wiping debris from their foreheads, pressing ears to chests. We've come this way before, but the fervor of their affection at every waking surprises me still. Benji and I died in the same city, around the same time, but in life, in Baltimore, both rooting for the O's, I never knew him. He delivered mail, had a cat named Ralph, and watched award shows because he liked to see hard work get recognized, liked the way elation looked on the winners' faces—naked and tearful. I ask him, "Why'd you become a mailman?"

"What's that matter?"

"I'm curious."

He stops, wringing out the hem of his shirt, and says, "It paid well. Well enough that I could get by just living with my cousin. Even put some money in savings. I didn't want to be one of those people working two jobs and never having a life."

When I try to get a glimpse of his face, he starts off in a different direction. I say, "So you got into it for the money."

"No, no, it wasn't that." He turns again, looking both ways at an intersection, searching the contents of each pool we pass. He says, "When I was a child, my mother would have these long conversations with everybody on the block. The milkman. The mailman. The women who worked at the laundromat below our apartment. She sat on the stoop giving out cigarettes to anyone who would stop long enough to smoke with her. It was lovely. Around Christmastime, she'd bake these thick sugar cookies for her friends. They were like little bricks, tasted just awful."

Children in swimsuits bump into us as they run through the channel. The youngest girl turns to apologize, and Benji smiles, says to run along. There is something diminished in his eyes, so I pat him on the shoulder, my fingers grazing the damp strap of his shirt. "No sign of champagne," Benji says. Then, "Surely there is someone here you're *dying* to meet." He grunts a laugh at his own joke.

I touch my fingers to the surface of an ocean. "Just Buckley, that singer I told you about." Benji furrows the skin on his forehead. I say, "He had this song, 'They're All Here For You.' I used to sing it to Andy sometimes."

"I can't say I know it."

"I'd sing it for you, but my falsetto is shit. She liked it though. It was the perfect song to tease her with. Guys were always hitting on her."

"In front of you?"

"Yeah. I mean, lanky Asian dude with a topknot, drumsticks poking out my back pocket. I'm not imposing. The kind of guys that came to our shows were pretty forward. I know what they were thinking—Oh, she's with him? Must be because she hasn't met someone like me."

We stop next to a pool of saltwater that's so clear it makes me thirsty. Benji looks me up and down. I can tell he's comparing himself to me, so I don't make eye contact, just drum triplets on the edge of the tank with the knuckles of my forefingers. "I'd be lying if I said I never let it make sense to me—Andy's relationship with me being a momentary stop on the way to settling down with someone who looked like her. But she used to just fuck with these guys," I say. "This one time, backstage, a dude sat on the other end of the couch, me on one side, Andy in the middle. He starts asking her about her work, where she lives, these first-date questions. Her hand was on my knee and everything. This guy didn't catch on. Or chose not to. I'll never forget, he asked her about the last place she traveled to, and she said Maui, then leaned over to me, basically shouting over the music. She said—Remember that? That was the time you took a shit on my chest."

"Wait, you did what?"

"Jesus, she was just fucking around. C'mon Benji."

"Well, I don't know."

"Do I look like that kind of person?"

"What does that kind of person look like?"

"Okay. Good point. But that's not what's important in *this* story. This dude couldn't hide his shock. But he tried to make like the comment hadn't bothered him. He leaned over, said, 'Oh, I've been to Maui. It's very pretty this time of year.'"

∼

I got this blazer at a secondhand store in Bethesda. I needed a suit, but I was broke, and Andy was always saying I'm the right size for thrifting—lean enough for the good pants, the best shirts. She'd done some sign work for the store, got them to set aside suits in my size, even got me a discount. I was the kind of steady who would wear a pair of shoes until the soles fell through, and Andy liked to plan for me, to find the ones to replace them. I'd asked her once if she enjoyed dressing me, and she said half the thrill was that I let her.

I keep the blazer on and lie back in the cold water, my breath buoying me. From the corner of my eye, I watch Benji slip as he climbs out of his tub, landing on his knee and laughing out a curse. Everything above us is white, and Benji reaches in and splashes me, saying, "C'mon, beautiful. Let's walk."

Roberta says, "I was beginning to think you two weren't coming." I wrap my arm around her back as she clears the tank. Steve brushes by us, leaving a trail of wet leaves. We're spinning the baby free from his bath, and I watch the water around Benji's arm stain pink as the minestrone from his shoulders washes off. This time Benji catches the boy, and Bon and the others come over and make funny faces to stop the child from crying while he heaves out his small lungs. Everyone is talking, and when I stand up straight, almost a head taller than this circle, I can hear murmurs of similar conversations in the distance. Benji bounces the baby on his forearm, and I tell him I'm going to walk alone today. I leave the blazer there, rip my sleeve, tie my hair, turning every six tubs, first left, then right.

As I approach her cell I know I've been here before, can recall, suddenly, the sensation of never wanting to return. Her brown hair curls to her waist on one side of her head, and on the other, it's knotted in the grating of the chain link suspended across half of her square. This entanglement happens sometimes—the things we were bound to in death coming with us. It's why so few of us are naked. These two women near me, Kathy and Mary Jo, both wake upside down, strapped to Oldsmobile seats. Mary Jo told me once that she pretends she's Houdini each time she unclasps her buckle. This girl whose hair is ensnared in chain link doesn't wrestle herself free. It's hard to tell her age while she's submerged in the flood-water, but judging by the folds of the corduroy jumper hovering about her, she can't be more than twelve. The last time I was here, a group of older men were calling through the water to her, reaching in and shaking the fence, trying to get her attention. Once I'd edged into the group, looking over their shoulders, it felt improper to walk off again, even as others peeked in then carried on, their conversations brightening before they were out of earshot.

We cannot cross over the threshold into another's vessel, and so there is nothing to do for her physically as she remains tangled under the floodwater. I prop myself on the glass, my chin on my forearms, focusing on the relative quiet in the space around her. Benji told me that, if you took off running in one direction, by the end of a cycle, you could make it back through a couple hundred years of drownings. He'd done it before, discovering the victims of the Middle Passage. "It's hurts to know," he said, "that we're capable of committing such ugliness." We didn't speak of it again, and I've always been ashamed of how quickly I decided never to go back and know it myself.

I reach over and shake the aluminum fence, put my mouth to the surface. It's hard to articulate words through the water, but what I shout is meant to sound like *please*. The water tastes metallic, and the blurred image of her shifts in the moss-green fluid. I reach toward her hair, toward the knots of it laced into the fence, but it's too far, so I settle against the lip, tell her I'm sorry for yelling. I say, "My friend Benji and I like to joke about names for the other afterlives. Heaven for your heart failure. Heaven for your blunt force trauma. Your internal bleeding." Behind me, a few cells back, women are singing. I don't know if she can hear me. I say, "But what if we're the only ones that get to linger? What if you have to drown to get to someplace like this? All the qualms I had with myself, with how I looked, with how people treated me, feel suddenly so foolish. It's lucky, having a little extra time. I want to make the most of it. Whatever that means." I place my palm on the surface, float it there, casting a shadow on the tank's floor. Honestly, I don't know if I blame her for refusing to rise. Maybe she had once. Maybe that was enough.

~

Tell me I'm pretty. Tell me I'm fun. Roberta says, "Not today. I could use a soak." We smile, then go save that baby. And another. We follow the crowd that gathers to free those who can't do so themselves. Then I get bored and take a left when everyone else goes right, and Benji says, "Did you and Andy fight often? Were you one of those couples?" I didn't think he'd follow me, but I tell him no, and then I'm steering and I keep straight. We nudge by a group of women with big hair and torn dresses, step by a row of children in loose-fitting Super Bowl T-shirts.

"It wasn't anything groundbreaking either. We just had a fight. Then I drank too much. If I weren't so tall, I'd probably still be alive. When I came off the stairs, I slipped, and the rail hit me in that part of the thigh where the nerves bundle together." Benji doesn't know what I'm talking about, so I punch him there, and his leg stiffens. While he kneads out his muscle with his knuckles, I think about hanging out after band practice, Jerome and me fucking around, trying to dead-leg each other. Every few intersections, Benji edges like he wants to turn. I feel like going forward.

We find him leaning against a tank, brown hair slicked back, boxers slung low across severe hips, his dirt-soaked clothes draped across the glass. I'm not quite sure it's him before we stop at his shoulder, but I say, "I'm a big fan."

Benji says, "You are?"

He shakes Benji's hand, then mine. He says, "It's been a while since I got recognized."

I say, "This is Buckley. The musician."

Benji smiles and nods, but I can tell he doesn't remember our conversation, so I say, "The singer we were talking about."

"Oh, the one you wanted to meet," he says. "Thump says your songs are beautiful. I'd love to hear one."

Buckley had been adjusting his underwear, following the awkward volleys of our conversation. He says, "Unfortunately, I'm retired. What are you gentlemen up to?"

"We're looking for a man who drowned in champagne," I say. The three of us glance down the length of the row, but there is no brass fluid glowing in the glass of a vessel.

"Well, tell me about yourself," Benji says. "It's always nice to meet new people."

Benji still smells like tomatoes and salt. I squirm at his eagerness, and it's been so long since I practiced embarrassment that it feels unnatural. Buckley scratches his head, saying with a chuckle, "I didn't realize how little I missed being interviewed."

"What's the harm in sharing a story or two?" Benji says. "I love hearing about other people's lives. What else are we supposed to be doing around here?" Benji raises his hands, palms up, then lets them fall to his side.

"You remind me of my uncle." Buckley looks at his bare feet, shins still caked in Mississippi River mud, and says, "He used to gather all my cousins up on holidays when he'd had a few and tell us stories, even if we didn't want to hear them. This one fable, growing up, I thought about it all the time. I tried to write a song or two about it, but nothing panned out." Benji asks if he can recall it, and Buckley stares somewhere above my shoulder. He said his uncle was in Vietnam, had fallen in love with a woman there, used to sneak away from base to stay with her when he wasn't on patrol. So while they fended off sleep, she told him fables about her village. At the dinner table, after the food had been cleared, Buckley's uncle would get drunk and retell them, rubbing his swollen knuckles with the bottom of a Budweiser. There were many stories, but Buckley's favorite went something like this:

> In the mountain above our village lived an old, radiant tiger, and we'd learned to hate it for its beauty. When the sun rose above the peak, shining over us, the tiger left its canopy and walked among our crops, its fur swollen a brilliant gold in the light. Legends said the cat was ancient, preserved in its health by the power of the sunlight. In recent years the harvest had grown thinner, and our men blamed the tiger, saying its pelt stole the sun's nurturing. Our elders told us the tiger was part of the village, that they'd settled in this land at the time of its birth. The tiger had protected our land from invaders in surrounding lands. But as we grew hungrier, a group of warriors gathered and stalked the mountain. They trapped the tiger in a cave, made a wall of spears and torches. Cornered, the tiger fought its way to freedom. But the next day, the survivors gathered again, chasing the injured cat to a cliff. And still it clawed its way back into the forest. On the third day, the last of the men assembled to

hunt, and the elders begged them to stay, that they shouldn't risk their lives. As they argued, the tiger lumbered into the village center, its fur streaked with wounds. In the ensuing battle, it killed half the remaining warriors before they got a spear into its heart. The children dug a grave along the river delta, and before nightfall the cat was buried. When the next harvest arrived, the rice grew thicker, the fruit weighed down the branches. We rebuilt wondering why the sun had chosen to bless the tiger and allow us to starve. Wondering what we had lost by killing it.

The three of us stand in a triangle. Benji rubs his hand on his chin, saying, "The splendor of nature—we were always destroying it."

"I'm not sure that's the moral of the story," I say. "The tiger was part of the village."

"So what do you think it means?" Buckley sets his elbow on the edge of the glass, and the contact sends a ripple across the brown river.

"They were in need, so they blamed the part of themselves they didn't understand, the part of the village they no longer saw the use in, even if it was essential in defining them," I say. "They thought the tiger was doing them harm. It was easy for them to hate it."

In the distance, I can hear someone splashing, and farther still, a woman calls out a name. Benji crosses his arms over his belly, and Buckley turns his back to us, leaning against his tank. I know I didn't pay enough attention to find my way back here. I know I will never get to ask him the questions that, in life, I wouldn't have gotten the answers to. But as I stare into the mire, I can't stop picturing the children digging that grave in the delta, their tan hands caked in earth, the sun setting fire to their black hair, so much like mine.

$\sim$

There is an instant before my body rises, before I break the surface and my throat clutches for air, when I am lying on the floor of my tub hugging my knees to my chest, all that dark water above. Here, I am closest to life, clinging to that final breathless moment when my body gave out. By then my brain was barely firing. The capillaries in my eyes ruptured, and in those explosions, I didn't see a grand image of my life, only the yellow lights dancing in the paint on my drum kit, Jerome's feet pigeon-toed about the microphone stand, Andy in the audience, looking out across the Bay, bobbing to the rhythm. Any movement would buoy me to the surface, so I keep still. Benji beats his fist to the edge of my pool. I can hear him call, "Thump," his voice deadened by the water. When he leaves, I concentrate on the image of Andy, her brassy hair tossing about her. We'd been friends since elementary school, but the night we got together, we were dancing in a Baltimore club. Growing up, I'd found her so charming, but until that moment, swaying through the night in celebration of her latest breakup, I hadn't mustered the nerve to do something about it.

On the boat, Jerome's voice was jaw and whiskey, doing his best Mick Jagger, coming out of the PA over my shoulder. The night was hot, and my thumbs were slick against the drumsticks as I dug into the hi-hat. The balls of my feet bounced on the pedals. I kept the band leashed to the back of the beat, driving through the chorus. As I raised my arm and whipped my wrist toward the crash—the song drifting back into the verse—the joint-loosening joy of life tipped in me, and I could feel every stomped foot in the crowd, every inch of the yacht shaking, every sway of the Chesapeake compelled by the beat in my kick drum. The set ended, and before I could start packing up, Andy said, "C'mon, handsome." She grabbed my wrist and dragged me through the crowd.

The host got a playlist going on the sound system, and as we disappeared into the belly of the yacht, Jerome said, "How do you think we did?"

He checked to make sure his date wasn't listening, and when he looked away, I punched him in the thigh, saying, "You saw them dancing." Then Andy pinched Jerome on the cheek and led me into the ship, past the waiters, the crew, all too tipsy to care about our intrusion.

We'd had sex in public before—in bathrooms at parties, in backseats after shows, too ready to be home to actually make the drive. So when she unbound my belt and hopped onto the table in that dim-lit storage room, I wasn't alarmed. What I wanted was to satisfy the taste for thrills that propelled her. I used to think that was why she liked me—my ability to join her in risk. It wasn't the first time we failed to use a condom either. She'd look me in the eyes, saying, "Don't you dare finish." It might've been that we drank too much free booze that night, trying to make up for the light pay, or that the chop kept rocking the table into the wall, tilting me toward her. She made a sound so low and intimate that when I opened my eyes to see her face soaked in amber light, I couldn't stop myself. She said, "Did you?"

"Fuck, I'm sorry."

The way she laughed helped soften my embarrassment. She hugged me, her arms over my shoulders, her hands gripping the length of my hair. She said, "I wondered what it would be like to date teenage you." I started to pull away from her, and she locked her fingers together behind my neck, said, "Stay. The damage is already done." She kissed me on the chin and pinched my hips with her thighs. I held her chest to me, could feel the confusing rhythm that her pulse layered in mine.

I said, "I can pick one up tomorrow. I'll pay for it."

"Sometimes you're too romantic for me."

"I'm just being practical."

"Don't be practical while you're inside me."

I touched my forehead to hers, dropped my hands to rest against the folds of her sundress, bunched across her hips. She said, "Would it be the worst thing to have a little Asian baby?"

"Don't fuck around."

"Jesus, why're you so ready to do away with it before it's even a problem?"

The room swayed. I said, "I just thought we were on the same page about this."

I was looking at the pair of moles on her sternum, and Andy tilted her head to try and meet my eyes. She said, "Just think about it for a second. Our beautiful little Asian baby."

"Stop doing that."

"Why is it so terrible to consider?"

"It's not. It's not that. Just stop qualifying it."

"You are Chinese. What else would it be?"

"It would just be our kid. *My* kid."

"It can't be *your* kid without being that."

"Is that why you want it?"

Under the deck, the feet stomping on the dance floor above sounded like they might cave the roof in. Andy slid away from me and pulled her skirt down around her knees. The current rocked my thighs into the edge of the table. She said, "Is that what you think?"

～

There is an instant before my body rises when I'm still sitting on the lips of death, making fists in the black water. I'm not sinking, just listing in the stomach of the Chesapeake. The pressure of the Bay pushes its fingers into my eardrums, the water past my throat, my stomach, my lungs. This is after the held-breath panic, that first swallow, and surrender. There is no boat, no coast or beach, pebble-strewn and gray. Up the way, that hand-me-down Corolla with its seats folded back will not be reloaded with my drums. I won't thank Andy for letting me drag her to another gig, and she won't tell me to stop apologizing for existing. I wonder if she ever had children, if she named one Theodore, even if he isn't mine, a thin strand of my thoughts reaching backward toward life, then

Thump! and the dull knock of knuckles to glass. I want just one more moment there, the image of Andy's curls tossing with the rhythm as she dances, but Benji won't leave, so I rise and heave and the water laminates my hair about my face, drops of it studding my eyelids. He says, "Where've you been?"

I fold my blazer, remove my shirt, climb free and gather a ponytail behind my head, wringing it between my palms. I watch Benji help Roberta clear from her bath and touch Steve on the scalp as he runs off to play. Jessica and Bon, each with a baby, walk arm in arm through the channel. Water runs from the tips of my hair past the small of my back, and Benji says, "Let's go somewhere."

He's asking me questions, but I don't feel like talking. We stop for a crowd of cruise-wreck victims to move through an intersection, and Benji says, "Have I ever told you about my route?" Pulling on the wet horsetail of hair that falls between my shoulder blades, I shake my head. He says, "I delivered for most of Roland Park—Cold Spring to the lake. My mom had us in Patterson when I was young. I was used to that kind of Baltimore, the only foliage matted with dog piss and stubbed-out cigarettes. Roland Park felt false to me. I mean, it's beautiful, don't get me wrong, all the grass and fat old trees, but you can feel the walls there, you know? You can't even hear the music of the streets just four blocks south. I didn't get into mail to schlepp around the suburbs, dropping letters in decorative mailboxes. I wanted to meet people. I wanted a neighborhood. The only people I ever saw were the kids playing in their yards.

"So one day, I park at the bottom of this cul-de-sac and deliver on foot. It was summer, and I was tired of being stuck in the van. It must've been eighty-five out. The sunlight playing in the trees was breathtaking. So I'm halfway back when I hear this little girl scream. It turns out the neighbor's Chow got out and was biting her on the ankle. The dog's muzzle was this terrible color red. I take off my shoe and I'm hitting it on the head, but it wasn't letting her go. She keeps screaming, so I gather my nerves up and reach into its mouth and pry its jaw off her ankle. Its teeth tore my fingers all up. By then, the girl's mother comes out of their house, and the Chow runs off. She's asking what happened, scooping her daughter up. It takes a while for us to feel safe again. We're standing on their porch and the daughter is just wailing. The mother thanks me, and the whole time, all I can feel is my fingers throbbing. I ended up getting thirty-six stitches over this. I kept picturing the dog spit mixing in my wounds. All I wanted to do was wash my hands off, so I ask if I can come in and use the bathroom. And sure, she let me."

Benji stops, leaning against a pond thick with algae. The wrinkles in his forehead darken as he dips his head. "But she paused first," he says. "I'm standing there with two palms full of blood, and she paused. Like she can't trust me. Just for an instant. I was in too much pain to let that settle in, but later. I don't know. It got to me."

When I put my hand on his shoulder, I can feel the dried soup crusted like sand to his skin. I tell him, "Hey, when she tells that story about the mailman who saved her daughter, or when that girl grows up and she talks about the scar on her leg—you know they'll leave that part out."

Then we're walking, and when we make a turn, the champagne is so bright it looks like the sun itself kneeling at our feet. An older man in a halter-top dress has a cigarette pinched between his lips and is spinning the wheel of the Zippo with his thumb. We lean over the glass, smelling the grapes, the too-sweet perfume of fermentation. The bubbles whisper as they break the surface. Benji closes his eyes and smiles. In the middle of the pool, a blonde wig floats. Turning, he extends his hand. "You must be Wilhelm."

Wilhelm takes Benji's hand, then runs his palm over the stubble on his scalp. Over his shoulder, I can see Roberta enter the channel, her hair folded onto her collar bone, and at her side,

Buckley is walking in nothing but his underwear and boots still thick with mud. He waves and says, "Hello, gentlemen."

They join our circle, and Benji turns back to Wilhelm. "Please, you must tell us about yourself. We've all heard so many stories about you."

Wilhelm takes the cigarette in his hand, regarding the soiled paper with a dissatisfaction that gives way suddenly to a chuckle and shake of the head—the kind of patience and grace reserved for mothers. Refitting it on his lip, he spins the metal wheel of the lighter with his thumb. He says, "I don't have any stories. I'm just waiting for the wick to dry."

Hung Do's Kung Fu

They've got me on the early shift at the bakery, pre-dawn: French loaves, dinner rolls, ciabatta, and rye, the shit no one eats until lunch or later. I have aprons all over the back of my car, dirty ones on the floor, clean ones on the seat. Under the fading moon, even the freshly washed folds of orange cloth are speckled with ash. I shake one out, not the cleanest—I want to save that for another day, a day with more potential. Today is Tuesday, a non-day that will mesh into the others spent rolling dough, throwing flour, breathing yeast; the cutting board, the oven, the cooling rack, then into paper wrappings and onto the truck. Not like a Thursday, when I pick my co-worker Lonnie up at 7-Eleven on my way downtown. She'll have two rolled cigarettes and ask, "You want one?" But I don't smoke—it makes me anxious—so she puts the other behind her ear, draped in the loose curls of her chestnut hair.

"You mind?"

"Go right ahead."

"I'm quitting. Well, I'm trying to."

We have this conversation every week. I imagine, in the summer, she'd crank the window down and let the moist air in, but it's still January, so she only cracks it the width of her finger and blows her smoke in kisses through the crevice. She runs back-up most shifts: sweeps the floor, restocks the saran wrap, stands around in her black Vans and loose coveralls only touching her chest and her hips. I'd done the same job for a year before they put me on the line. All morning, we talk about the stupid shit we've done with our lives, those silly little tales that, if you think about it, somehow ended up with us here. It's my turn today, so I'm telling her about this time I left a girl in my class a secret admirer's note, a story I've probably already told her before.

"Torrie had this gorgeous tan skin, big green eyes. She had a good sense of humor, too. She could give it as good as she got it, so no one really messed with her. But you know how kids are: when you like someone, you tease them. So I would have a go at her during lunch, at gym, pretty much anytime I got a chance."

"What about?"

"There wasn't much. About the way she wore ponytails a lot. Said glasses made her look like an old lady."

"Hah," she says, moving a rack onto a cart. "What'd she say about you?"

"Well shit, it wasn't exactly hard," I say. "Called me button nose. Called me short. Squinty eyes. Et cetera."

Lonnie says, "Poor little you."

"I was okay with it, I think. I mean it was nice just being on her radar."

I pull the last batch out, wrap them up. I start cleaning my station while Lonnie mops.

"So Valentine's rolls around, and I write her this poem and put it with a carnation in her desk. I had to walk to school really early so no one saw me do it."

"You thought that would work?"

Tossing the dirty rags in the hamper, I say, "Well shit. I was a kid. Anything was possible."

When we're off at one, and I'm taking her back uptown, I ask her to get a drink or see a movie. She always says she's busy, has to see her mother, or maybe she doesn't want to go out in her work clothes and doesn't know if she will be awake enough to meet up with me later. Then she thanks me for the ride. I'll shoot her a half-smile because I only half-care. That's the thing about being tired: disappointment only festers a moment before it falls apart. It doesn't build up long enough to make a difference. I go home and shower, drink a coffee, throw darts. I lie down, and instead of sleep, I do crosswords. I never finish them, though, cause I won't let myself look at the key. Eventually, I figure, I'll get literate enough that I can go back and finish the old ones, but I've already done once-throughs on the whole book, so I turn on the TV and watch anime. And then I'm tired, but I can't sleep because I know I haven't seen this episode of Trigun, which plays from eleven to two in the morning. It's that sad episode right near the end of the season, and I keep missing it. It's been ages since I've slept a full night, but I nod off after one and I'm up at four for another Wednesday or whatever day that isn't Thursday and Friday—the shifts I pick up Lonnie. Those days just go faster.

⌒

The big loaves get two scores across the top before another run of flour on the prep slab, then the oven. The ciabattas get three-against-one this month, two-against-none at other times—who knows why. Pressed up against the stainless steel table, I could be a machine if not for this little bundle of muscle beating drops of inconsolability through my veins: discontent at the person I have become versus what I used to be. Where did the passion to embarrass myself, to write a love letter go? Now, I'm twenty-nine, rolling dough into cylinders with no friends, no interruptions to my routine. But it's one, and all that grief blends together, sifts between my fingers, disappears in the friction between my palms. I shape the dough. I scrape it up. I set it next to the roll that came before it. As I'm lying down at the end of the day, that grief reappears in the hiss of air rushing out of my pillow, sings me, not a lullaby, but the song of a snake charmer, lulling me into a trance.

⌒

It's Thursday and Lonnie has cut all her hair off. She's smiling. When she gets in the car, it takes everything intelligent left in me not to run my simian hand across the top of her head. She's already got one cigarette perched on her chapped lips. She offers me the other.

Today I say, "Yeah, why not."

The first inhale tastes shitty and makes me cough, and the four years since I'd quit disappear with the smoke rolling out the window. In the parking lot, I can't tie my apron while smoking, so she ties it for me. When she's done, she brushes the remnants of old flour off my shoulders. The whole thing is very sweet, and I say, "Aren't you sweet." She snickers. I say, "Let's get wings and go to the duckpin place. I know you're into that."

"I am. But it's my thing. I like going alone."

"Then something else. Whatever you want."

"You going to beg, too?"

"I'm getting pretty close."

She stomps her cigarette out, pulls the top of her coveralls over her shoulders, waits for me to hold the door open. "I'm not in a good place right now. I don't know. Why waste your time? Plenty of other girls."

"Yeah, but you get how it is—the weird schedule—I don't have to explain it to you."

"I'm sure someone else could get you."

"I'm a late-twenties baker who isn't *technically* a baker since all I do is follow a recipe. Who could understand that?"

She puts on her latex gloves. "Well when you put it like that, you sound weird."

"I *am* weird. Don't pretend that you don't like it." I punch into the computer then step aside so she can do the same.

She says, "Get to work, Hung."

It is, I suppose, slightly important that my name is Hung Do, a lightning rod for xenophobic commentary and pun humor. *How do Hung Do? Not so Hung Dude. How much rice can Hung Do Chew? Hung Do's Mu Shu Tofu. Welcome to Hung Do's Kung Fu, how're you?* I have heard it all, from old friends and lesser people. I almost find any new quips entertaining. Nothing stuck better than *Hung Do's Kung Fu*. When I was younger, my friends wore out the joke to the point that people I hadn't met knew me by the phrase, to the point that my closest friends thought it would be endearing and *awesome* if I actually opened up a dojo, to the point that I took Wushu classes once a week for two years. I even enjoyed the order to the operatic style: the forms we had to memorize, the stances constructed of perpendicular limbs, how every movement was an arrow falling from the sky—a slow arc that landed with a crack. When I got passed up for green belt my third time, I realized it was because of my boyish physique. I was too square with only a hint of muscle, couldn't perform correctly. And like that, I gave it up. By the time I had grown into something more concrete, I knew it wasn't my dream unrealized, but someone else's. I'd never considered going back.

Lonnie doesn't care about all of that. She has her own shit to sift through. Her kid is with her on the weekends, a little girl whom she had ten years ago, kept her out of college. Girl's father comes around every now and again to start things back up, *blows her mind*, then pushes her to the point they tear into each other. Lonnie takes him back because she wants stability for her girl. That's what she tells me, at least, while she's changing the liner in my trash can and refilling the wax paper. I can't comprehend any of it.

Those days, the ones when he moves back out, she wears too much foundation, cakes it on, aggravates her acne for a week. The car rides are quiet then, and I never ask her out because I'm such a gentleman. I'd like to say that thinking about her cleaning off all that makeup, wiping off all that lipstick, revealing a split lip and a mouse under her right eye, I'd like to say that's what kept me up. But by the time I'm home, all I can think about is rubbing my fingers against the flanks of her head, feeling the roughness of her stout hairs against my thumbs. Maybe if I took care of myself, I could fall asleep, so I do, I take care of myself, but in a way that has nothing to do with my health. I'm in bed at eleven. I fall asleep sometime after one.

At four in the morning, on a Friday—a good day—I'm at 7-Eleven, but Lonnie isn't leaning against the newspaper stand that she would have just rolled her cigarettes on. I wait ten minutes, then go to work where the boss says that she called out, said she needs a week off. He tells me to pick her up next Thursday if that's not a problem.

All the days of that week are tedious. More flour, more yeast, my hands can't forget the touch of the roller, and I'm thinking that it would be heroic to drive around her neighborhood, see if she's there, find out if there's anything I can do to help. When I get the resolve together, or when I think I have it, it's already midnight, and I don't know five letters for *The Right Honourable Romantic Poet* even though the second letter is *y*. It's the first time I've seen this episode of Trigun again because I'm too tired to pay attention. I'm never paying enough attention.

~

I get to 7-Eleven a little bit early, buy two coffees, wait for her to round the corner. She already has her uniform square and zipped up. I hand her the styrofoam cup and some rolling papers and say, "You okay?"

"I'm fine. Just had the flu is all." She takes the tobacco from her pocket, rolls two with ease, licks the ends. Her fingernails are chewed off.

"You get into it?"

"No, just had the flu. I'm okay now. You want one?"

"Sure."

She doesn't say anything on the ride in, but looks at her cigarette like she distrusts it, chucks it out when it's still half good. On the drive home, I let her out unencumbered by my advances and wait for her to thank me for the ride before I head home.

Standing outside the passenger window, she says, "That it?"

"Thought I would give you a little bit of time, since you're sick."

"Don't change it up," she unzips her coveralls and pulls her arms through. Her chest practically heaves into the window. "Tell me what you want to do."

On the spot, it's hard to feel anything close to confident when coated in thin layer of sweat and confection. "Let's get a beer or something. Whatever you want."

She flashes a look like she just lost the lottery. "Pick me up at five."

Under the heavy flow of the faucet, I shower for what feels like hours but ends up being sixteen minutes. I put on a pair of jeans I bought but never wore—never had a reason—a favorite T-shirt, and a crew neck sweater that makes my shoulders look broad. I lie on the bed for a few hours, set an alarm just in case, then stare at the chipped paint on my ceiling.

I'm wondering how much paint costs when we order another pitcher at the duckpin place. I've never seen her outside of work. She's wearing cut offs over tights and a black henley that sticks to her. When she bowls, her hips swivel like she's about to come apart. The beer goes through me, makes me look like I'm out of breath. When I get back from the bathroom, she's drying her neck with a napkin.

"You getting sleep yet?" she says. I sit on the plastic bench and she's next to me, pigeon-toed with her bottom lip sucked in. She puts her thumb, wet from her beer's condensation, on the bag under my eye. She says, "You just need to be properly tired."

It's ten and we're slow dancing to Johnny Cash, then Etta James, then Al Green, and I'm filling her ear with everything I think she wants to hear. I tell her I want to be there for her. I want to provide for her. And her kid. I've never been that responsible, but how hard can it be? I can make it all that much easier.

She says, "Why?"

"To help you. You know," I stutter, "to see you grow."

"What makes you think that is what I'm looking for?"

The bowling alley is underlit with orange and reds bulbs that paint the walls a Kool-Aid tinge, and I'm too drunk or lazy to read the scorecard. I know I haven't won a game. Around eleven, she suggests we run away. "It would be so much simpler to just go. South America," she says. "Fuck it, I don't even want my shoes back."

"What about Brittany?"

"What about her?"

It was the wrong thing to ask, but the moment isn't all-the-way broken.

"Nothing good is easy. Not anymore," she says. "Or maybe nothing good is fun."

I can't remember the last time someone else was in my boxy flat. It feels big, but only because of the lofted ceilings. The exposed brick does nothing but drive up the rent. We're fucked up. I think I tipped the cab driver too much. I could've probably driven. She says she likes my place, says it's not pretentious, that my sink half-full of dishes and the bed unmade are honest touches. She says I'm not trying too hard.

The tattoo on her ribs could be a lotus flower or an octopus, but it's too dark to tell. I only have one lamp in my bedroom. We're kissing and for some reason, I'm worried I forgot to pay the electric bill. Her shaved head is velvet against my palms. She's pulling on me, tugging, pleading with it, promising things I've thought about countless times—acts I've imagined while making deals with myself. But I'm too drunk. I can barely feel my toes much less the parts whose muscles don't connect directly to my brain. Then she's curled up in a ball, not sad, just tired, she says. I tell her I didn't mean to let her down, but she says it's fine, really, she's just tired. But I won't have it, so I pry her knees apart, bury my nose in her stubble, knead my tongue until my bottom teeth cut up the underside and it feels like it might fall out of my mouth. She's too drunk, though, says she won't be able to finish. She wraps us up the wrong way in the covers. We have to be at work in a little under four hours. I'm still messed up. The walls vibrate.

She rolls over onto her stomach so that the only thing touching me is her bare shoulder and her face is bunched against the pillow. She says, "Tell me about the poem. I need something to fall asleep to."

"You sure you want to hear it again?"

She kisses the side of my head.

I pull my boxers on and close my eyes with her, hoping to talk myself to sleep.

"What'd you say?" she whispers.

"You sure you want to hear it again."

"No, in the poem."

"Oh. I don't remember."

"C'mon." Her fingers graze my thigh.

"It was kid shit. I was like twelve or thirteen. I probably wrote about the same things I teased her about, but truthfully, saying the things that felt sort of overwhelming, you know? How her eyes were so pretty. How her hair was so golden. Her smile—I can almost see it. But we were kids. I wasn't even looking for anything. I mean, what could I have been looking for? I guess it just felt nice to tell her something that wasn't mean. To tell her how I actually meant to feel."

In the prisms of color that dance on the back of my eyelids, I see the ghost of Torrie: that hair with its ageless luster, soaking in the noontime sun. In a breath, I'm a child again, bowl cut and baby fat, hovering like a moth at the edge of a porch lamp, doing everything I can to be close to her without it appearing like that's what I want. "It's such a strange idea, isn't it? That something so pure can somehow be attainable."

The remembrance of that gentle wanting stirs me under the blanket. I reach over Lonnie, touch her on her ribs. I say, "Hey, are you still up for it?" But she's sputtering into the pillow, her pale back billowing as she breathes. So I go back to thinking about middle school and the only poem I ever wrote, about how she read it with the flower clung to her chest. From my desk, in the corner of the room, I saw the fluorescent light glint off her eyes as they absorbed each word. Then, the reality of my chicken scratch hand-writing started to show under the sentimentality. Torrie, along with a couple of her friends, went around, comparing the note with the pages of various boys' notebooks in the class. I got up and went to the bathroom, but when I got back, they were hovering there, the three of them, standing at each end of my desk. When Torrie spoke, she stuck her hip out and crossed her arms. The poem was on my desk. "Hung Poo, did you write this?"

I didn't regret the note, but I was too chicken-shit to take credit. I fended them off for a while, told a few lies, but after class, Torrie approached me by my locker. She said, "Look, it really was a sweet letter."

I didn't look, just grabbed a few books and stuffed them into my backpack.

"It was, really. It's just that I'm not supposed to like you."

I put a strap over my shoulder. "What do you mean?"

"Well you know Patricia, right?"

She was talking about her best friend, one of the girls who had just stood around my desk. She was tall with limp black hair and slender features.

"Patricia says you're cute. So I wouldn't be a great friend if I did that to her, would I?"

"Did what?"

"I don't know. Liked you, I guess."

Then she was gone, and I tried my best to digest what she had said over the excitement that, even if she didn't like me, someone might. The idea emerged out from beneath a scab, new skin breathing air for the first time, and before the end of the day, my fascination was diverted to Patricia's lithe smile. But I found out quickly that Patricia had no such feelings and had no clue why I would be under that impression—that it was all just another joke by Torrie, to give it out as good as she got it.

Lying on my bed with Lonnie blowing air out her half-open mouth, I realize it wasn't the prank that mattered but what that joke had reflected in me. The cracks in the paint above me grow as slow as the hour hand on a clock. If I left right now, I could be at the beach before dawn. My friends and I, we used to act like we were heading to school early, then meet in the parking lot behind the library and pack into someone's car. We'd get to the beach mid-morning and drink until dinnertime. I miss the drive: the way the plastic handles of Russian vodka beat the walls of the trunk, the way buying a cup of coffee under the smeared dawn sky made me feel like an adult, and after its warmth faded, how it felt like soy sauce on my tongue. When it got too cold to lie out in the sand, a couple of us stuck to our Friday truancy, found basements or parks to horse around in, but the bulk of my friends would get diligent in the winter, making up for all those grades they missed. I'm not sure why I was surprised when I didn't graduate, got held over for summer classes, missed that first semester at UMBC. I'm not sure why I never made it back, never caught up to them. Now, I can't help but feel callow. I can't stop pitying myself. I can't sleep.

～

The alarm goes off a half hour before our shift. I ask her if she wants to shower the night off and she suggests, in a mumble, that we call out, then rolls over, puts her knee on my thigh. Through all of my wallowing, I've been waiting for this, so I push her onto her back and place my hand at the delta between her legs, pressing my palm against her. All those immature mistakes well up in me, push against her hip, vanish behind five minutes of levity, and then, as I'm huffing the space between her shoulder and the pillow, they reappear to coat my insides, forming a cast as I fade back into something more dispassionate and cold. Lonnie moans into my ear, "Again."

Her voice reaches at something off in the distance, something beyond me. When she opens her eyes, she seems surprised to see my face, then shifts her hips so that I roll off of her. We're facing each other on the bed, slightly bent at the waist so that our toes are almost touching. When she adjusts the elbow under her cheek, I find myself mirroring her movement.

"What I said last night—"

"I know."

"I want you to know I meant it."

"I know."

When I get out of the shower, she's not in bed. She's not in the kitchen getting a glass of water or in the half bathroom washing her face. She isn't standing on the side of the road with two cigarettes or in the break room getting ready for her shift. I look for her in bars, grocery stores, in reflections. I'll turn, and bend, and change, but she is somewhere more concrete—a life I don't know how to realize—somewhere I'll never reach.

↶

Clean for Him the Ashes

I remember watching the Cotton family's kitchen burn, felt only a ripple of urgency. Knew it was the kitchen because the houses on this stretch are all the same split-levels built north of Ellicott City, the semi-rural bit just past 70—two main avenues laced together by branches of side streets, neighborhoods pocketed along them. I kept waiting for the flames to reach out like arms through the windows, but there were just these little tips of orange licking the gutter. Our plots were far enough apart that the heat didn't warp my siding, but the pungent smell of that old wood burning, the paint peeling, felt toxic, jarred me from an otherwise peaceful Monday night.

Fire fighters got it out in five. I had my face in the blinds, shifted to see the Cottons—father, mother, two boys—standing shoeless in the grass. It was warm for a September evening, but they huddled, heads tipped skyward as the tail of the smoke crept up past the alder trees lining our backyards. The Chief handed Mr. Cotton a phone, and he just stared at it like he was waiting for a call, didn't dial, gave it back to the Chief when he was done talking to his crew. The crowd of neighbors gathered on the opposite curb began to thin as the trucks pulled away, and I went back to dusting my living room.

My things were neatly organized, every object with a place. I've got a workshop in my garage where I refurbish the beat-up antiques I find in thrift stores, selling some, keeping the ones with good wood that's still breathing—two walnut end tables around my couch, oak shelves now full of DVDs, a secretary in the corner with a bottle of Lagavulin on it. This time of day, the amber fluid catches the last bit of sun reflected from the mirror in my foyer, bending it into a blade on the carpet. The crickets started up, their whine carrying under it a slow, choked pulse—Mrs. Cotton's sobs—and I suddenly couldn't see my possessions without also seeing them on fire, so I grabbed some TV dinners and my micro-wave and walked them over. Told myself it wasn't sympathy. When I was twenty-three, I fell into some life insurance and quit the engineering program at Hopkins to open my hardware shop. I figured they'd come to me for the repair eventually, might as well make my way to the money.

From the front door, there was no damage to see, could just feel the thick air as it moved out the open windows. Mr. Cotton hung bed sheets to contain the soot in the kitchen. I stood in the crux of their home, the bottom of the stairs where the living room, the dining room, the burnt kitchen all met, pretending like I didn't hear Mrs. Cotton as she repeated things like, "Just our luck," and, "I can't do this. I'm too tired for this," digging her thumb into the palm of her other hand. Their boys were still in elementary school, acted like the fire was just another one of those things that hap-pens—Christmas, summer vacation, a snow day—couldn't get their attention from the TV as they lay on their bellies scraping their forks in the plastic trays. I nudged the older one with my boot, told him to get his mother some water and a plate. Mr. Cot-ton held the sheet so I could pass.

It'd been a small electric fire. Didn't burn long enough to dam-age the frame, just ate up everything leading to it—the drywall, the wiring, insulation, and on the outside, visible through a small hole between the windows across from the sink, the siding. The smoke left gapped black lines like jail bars up and down the paint. I took the circular from their breakfast table and doubled it over, began listing materials for the repair, said I'd be by after I closed the shop tomorrow, would help him get it settled. He could pay me back in installments. Mrs. Cotton stood beside him in the doorway. She muttered, "What's another loan, right?"

He said, "You know it's going to take me a while to pay you back."

I said it was fine, as long as he stayed intending to repay it. Asked him if he had tools, and he said a hammer and some screwdrivers—told him I'd just bring mine over.

~

My shop was just off the main stretch of town where the Baptist church punctuated two strip malls and a Safeway. Business had been steady, but I'd learned early on that if I sold a hammer for seventeen, I only got to pocket eight, and I wasn't willing to split that, so the shop was only open if I was in it. Nights, I did repairs for people around town. It'd gotten to the point where I didn't have a conversation with someone unless it was about the work. In their eyes, I'm sure the shop and me were inseparable, and I was fine with that, didn't mind being known for what I could do with my hands, didn't mind making money off of that. I thought a lot of a person's real worth came through sweat, the knowledge of a sore back, a history of callouses. Maybe not all the value of a man, but the only part that I wanted to be familiar with, so that Tuesday I said, "Get the lead out," to the Cotton boys as they dawdled with my tool boxes, told them just to lug them over and set them down while I got to helping Mr. Cotton unload my pickup.

Out front, I drank a glass of water while the older Cotton boy rode his bike in circles on the driveway. The seat was a little low for him. Younger one poked around the tools with a look on his face like someone had lied to him. He said, "You don't have a monkey wrench?"

I took one of the red tools from the case, a smaller size, hefted it in my hand once, the metal catch rattling. He said it was a funny name for *that*, and what's it do? So I went to his older brother who was watching now, adjusted the wrench to the bolt under the seat, loosened, raised it, tightened it back. The younger boy was struck, a little teary, asked why I would go and do something like that. He disappeared into the house as Mrs. Cotton came out. Older boy told me they shared the bike and I had made the seat too tall for his brother, wanted me to lower it again. I handed him the tool, asked him if he saw how I did it. I told him to keep it, if it was okay with his mother.

"Jude, that's too kind of you," Ms. Cotton said. She looked more collected than yesterday, still in her work clothes, a blouse and slacks. She was the secretary at a law office in Catonsville, told me that a couple years prior when they moved in. Back then, I ran over one of the boys' action figures with my lawnmower. Those kids were always sprawled out in the yard, throwing their toys in a sort of plastic warfare. She had come to my door, crying boy two steps back, said, "Could you at least replace it?" Before I shut the door on them, I asked if she would've replaced the blade on my mower. Told her if they stayed off my grass, it never would've happened. We hadn't spoken since.

Standing in their yard now, I wanted to say something clever or blunt, something like *It's not really kindness if it's needed*, or *Well it's just honest work on credit—don't thank me too much*, but I couldn't look her in the face long enough to make a comment like that stick. She was a pretty woman, brown eyes that caught shine, but it wasn't her appearance, it was something about her exhaustion that made me fall silent. I just smiled, and I hated smiling, always felt a bit crooked on my face. My mother used to say a smile like mine could make the world take a knee. I didn't want that power. And it wasn't entirely a selfless thing either—local owner of the hardware store patching up a family's home might drum up business for me. Goodwill sells. Every dollar spent was two coming back.

A couple in their Sunday best got out of a car just parked by the mailbox, produced a bag of dry goods from their trunk. They looked confused as they inspected the front of the house, said, "We heard what happened. We wanted to help." Mrs. Cotton invited them in behind us.

Went over the order of repairs with Mr. Cotton. He was starting to show his age—slim in the appendages, the neck, but with a little weight in the stomach, clothes a bit too big for him, a spot on the scalp where the hair was thin. I just turned thirty-four, figured he must be a decade older. He, too, had good eyes, and a boyish grin that underlined them, made truth something Mr. Cotton had no problem showing, hell of a time hiding—not a bad quality for a real estate agent.

"But the market," he said to me while we got set up, "just isn't like it was."

The man in the tie shot glances past the curtain now pulled to one side so we could get the supplies from the dining room. Mr. Cotton and I tied rags over our mouths, put on goggles, hefted hammers. The other man leaned his head past the threshold before I lowered the sheet. He said it didn't look *too* bad. I showed Mr. Cotton the spots in the drywall we needed to remove. As the couple left, they kept reassuring, "We'll keep you in our prayers."

Ash spilled to the floor as we beat on the burnt wall, ripping out loose panels and tossing them out the back door into a trashcan. I double-checked the frame, removed the faulty hub that sprang the fire, ran my hands along the panels. As I pinned down new wiring, more and more visitors knocked on the door, spoke to Mrs. Cotton, glanced around the bed sheet, Mr. Cotton raising a gloved hand in an exhausted wave.

Late, we swept out the kitchen and hung a tarp over the opening. I offered Mr. Cotton a beer, but he said he needed to shower and get to bed, so I stood between our two homes, watched the wind tickle the blue plastic on the back of their house. The light in their bathroom came on, and Mrs. Cotton washed her face in the sink, ran her hands under the water, pinched her tear ducts, then, looking at herself in the mirror, she shook her head and flashed a smile before she got to soaping her hands. And I went inside, picked the dirt from under my nails, fell asleep in the center of the bed, telling myself that I was her relief.

~

Wednesday, I taught Mr. Cotton how to get the insulation into the wall without making a mess of the pink fibers. Outside, we placed new panels, hung and bolted the siding, worked long past dusk fixing the gutter. I narrated each step, unsure if he was absorbing it. But there was concentration in his expression, bags deepening, brow pulling in confirmation, nods and *mhms*. The visitors became less frequent, but the phone kept ringing. Mrs. Cotton gave thanks and repeated the story about the toaster outlet sparking, catching their wall on fire, kept reassuring the caller that they were okay, that they didn't need anything else, just had to pay for the repair. I was perched on the top of the ladder, tightening the new length of gutter, the lantern on the roof casting my shadow across the backyard. Mr. Cotton stood below holding screws, and I said he sure had a lot of friends. He seemed to misunderstand, but then nodded, said, "They're from our church."

Mrs. Cotton made a dinner of ham and cheese sandwiches, sliced apples. We sat on the living room floor, careful not to dirty their couch, and the phone rang again. Mrs. Cotton exhaled heavily, put her glass of soda down. When she came back, I commented that it must be nice to have a congregation that cared, and the Cottons' eyes became fixed on a spot on their plates. I asked how long they had been going. They said since their first was born, Mrs. Cotton's mother had insisted on a baptism, didn't go that regularly, but they had been lately, needed the help. Things had been thin. Mr. Cotton said it was a responsibility, a trade-off, couldn't take without giving back, and I figured he was talking about God, so I gave a firm nod before I realized he'd meant money. I finished my sandwich, rarely ate pork but I didn't want to be rude. Mrs. Cotton took the kids upstairs to help with their homework. I carried the ladder back to my garage.

Slept shaky that night, always did when there was work to finish. My body ached from armpits to hips, but I could find no peace, no dreams, just fits of rest between moments of dozing, half awake, listening to the cicadas and the crickets, watching the streetlights resting beams against my curtains. Lying there, I couldn't unsee how Mrs. Cotton turned her head away when her husband spoke about the help their church gave them. Her downturned lips and a flare in her nostrils—the slightest edge of her shame.

~

Thursday, we fitted the drywall, sanded and sealed it. I measured the portion of damaged counter, and then Mrs. Cotton came into the kitchen, said that the monthly seminary meeting was that night, that one of them should go. He raised his hands, dirty white from the work, "Honey, you know I would."

"I know, I just—" she put her hands on her hips, "It's okay. I'll go."

Mr. Cotton got the boys fed and settled in their rooms, came down in time to help me finish the sealing. Then we couldn't continue while it dried, so we carried the garbage to the curb for collection. I was on the last beer, offered him one, and he said sure, came to my house and stood in my living room as I grabbed two from the fridge. He had his hands in his pockets, leaning toward the bottle of scotch on the secretary, its plastic-sealed lip. "Nice bottle," he said. "Saving it for something?"

Said that I wasn't saving it, just had no cause to crack the label it yet. It was too big a purchase to use on just anything. I'd bought it when I opened the store and intended it for the next milestone. Hadn't figured out what that could be. He said I was young for all this—the house, the shop. Against the backdrop of my organized possessions, he looked untidy and raw from work. The condensation from the beer can wet the pale sealant on my palms. Told him I'd had some help with insurance money when my mother passed away. He said he was sorry to hear it.

~

Friday, the boys played outside, and we stripped the drywall, got it ready for paint. Mrs. Cotton stirred the primer dressed in sweatpants and one of her husband's old button down shirts, sleeves rolled to her elbows. She brought a boombox out of the family room, put on the Beach Boys' *Greatest Hits*, poured the white paint into a tray and began strumming it with a roller while we taped down the catches. For the topcoat, they picked a soft, matte green called winter grass. Mrs. Cotton shoved a bag of popcorn into my hands, said, "Jude, we can do this part." They were good at painting. When they'd gotten together, before the kids came, they used to repaint their apartment every year.

"We always needed some change," she said. "And it was cheaper than buying new furniture." She placed a hand on her husband's shoulder as she passed behind him. I chewed the kernels, sat on a bucket, resting my back. They bopped to the music, and I laughed when Mr. Cotton slipped into falsetto for *God Only Knows*. Told me stories about their life together, one of them starting it, the other, brush still, listening until they recollected it and broke in to finish. They'd met as sophomores at McDaniel. Mr. Cotton almost dropped out before he met her, planned to return to Virginia for cheaper tuition. She said he should've gotten out while he had the chance. It was funny how they shared memories of the years they dated, each carrying a portion, and together, hoisting them to the surface. I couldn't recall a time when I experienced such unrehearsed balance.

While the primer dried, the boys left for a sleepover at their friend's house. We sat around on the floor in the living room drinking the last of my cheap beer, the CD restarting. Mrs. Cotton asked me about my family, and there wasn't much to it, not an interesting story—mother raised me by herself, was a nurse, worked a lot. My father was never around, but that wasn't so unusual back then, lot of my friends were in the same situation. I didn't feel wounded by it. Besides, I worshipped my mother, was alive because of her effort, even if that meant I grew up alone.

Told them a story about how I used to jump on my bed after a bath. Don't remember why I did it, but it was fun, and when my mom was on call, when she actually had to go in to cover a night shift, this is what I'd do when there was nothing but the news on. So, I was jumping, probably shouting some song, and I landed weird in the middle of the bed, heard this crack—flicked my can when I told this part—and the middle of my bed sunk in. I'd broken one of the support boards. Mrs. Cotton said her boys did that once. I smiled my crooked smile, said I was petrified my mom would find out. She did enough, didn't need to be worrying about fixing my bed, so I shoved toys under it, held it up, made it look normal until I figured out how to mend it.

Mrs. Cotton said, "You must have had a ton of toys."

I hadn't expected her to break into the story there. It took a moment to decongest the rest of it from where it got hooked in my throat. I said, "I, uh, guess I never really thought about that. Suppose I did." I ended up taking a piece of fence post that broke off the neighbor's a while before, hammered about thirty nails between it and the beam. It still made me laugh, how little I knew about wood back then, how little I understood sturdiness. I described how mangled the repaired beam looked, like a weapon, nail heads all uneven and jutting out.

Mrs. Cotton said, "It must have been tough on her, raising you alone."

"We have a hard enough time between the two of us," Mr. Cotton finished.

I said, "We got by." Our family was small and she worked hard. Mrs. Cotton asked if my mom ever found out about the bed, and I said, "I don't think she ever knew the truth, no."

Mrs. Cotton nodded. I felt a little off, didn't mean the story to be somber.

Mr. Cotton grinned, said, "Bet you never jumped on the bed again."

I said, "No sir." He was still smiling, but his eyes were vacant. They stood up and started on the first coat. I went home and tried to relax but I kept wondering if I really had it in me back then to mend that support post, if I actually could have done it, instead of blaming it on the cheap bed, instead of demanding a new one. Ten years old, all fists and high-pitched yelling. Had to have what the other kids had, always demanding more and more. I wish it had been in her to say *No*.

～

Saturday, I stopped by on my way to work. They'd done two coats, then the trim. It looked good. Only the counter and the floor were left, said we would get to it, and I closed the shop early, arrived as Mrs. Cotton was coming back from Bible study with the boys. Older one whined, didn't understand why they had to start going again, plucking his clip-on tie from his collar. Mr. Cotton pulled up the ruined tiles while I adjusted the cut on the new counter, went to the backyard, trimmed it to size. I held it to the old one. The color didn't match perfectly, but Mr. Cotton wiped his brow on his forearm, said, "It's fine. It's good. Really."

After dinner, I got to scrubbing the floor with a steel brush, Mr. Cotton taking a break, the sheet in the doorway gone. The house had almost healed. A knock at the front door, and Mrs. Cotton answered while Mr. Cotton sipped his beer. When he heard the voice, he stiffened and placed it on the new counter on his way to the living room. I didn't pay much attention to the conversation, was just getting to the last bit of ash hidden in the corner under the cupboards. I saw, first, black oxfords, glaring bright under the work lamps, almost like patent leather, but just shined up recently. Then slacks, gray sweater, clergy collar like a baby tooth in the middle of an empty mouth. I pushed myself up to my knees, dried my face on my T-shirt, could feel the air touch the sweat on my stomach. He had pockmarks in his cheeks that reminded me of old cork board with the staples ripped out, thin eyes, a tuft of white hair. He raised his hands to his sides, "This is good work. This is *good* work."

Mrs. Cotton introduced him as Pastor Mills. Didn't make it to my feet as he came over to shake my hand, felt a little odd kneeling in front of him, so I spoke little, just said I was giving my neighbor a good rate, not much else to it. I've never been good at carrying on, not with work underfoot. I asked if he would excuse me to get back to it, needed to finish up so I could get some rest, wasn't really true though, I just felt a little imposed upon, this presence suddenly overhead, watching my hands.

In the living room, seated in a circle, the Cotton family and their pastor talked about faith and healing. The Pastor said there was no healing without faith and no faith without prayer. I scrubbed, the shins of my pants wet, my hands rubbed raw, my lower back hot and sore—I wanted to grind my callouses to the bone. Kept saying the word in my head again and again. Prayer. Prayer. And I had when she was gone. I had, but it could never give her back all those hours of overtime I'd shamed her into, always wanting, couldn't erase the days I ignored her as a teenager, out marauding at parties with my friends. Prayer wouldn't tell her what I now understood. It would never get me even. I excused myself for the night, shook no hands.

⁓

Sunday, my shop was closed. When I first took it over, I was open seven days a week, but no one came in on the Sabbath. I'd stand at the counter watching families cross from the parking lot to the church, white shirts and khaki pants, red ties and sundresses. At nine this morning, Mr. Cotton was knotting his tie when he opened the door, said, "Jude, we didn't expect to see you so early."

I wanted to finish up the floor, finish the repair, be done by lunch.

"It's just that we can't miss services." His collar was uneven. "But you should come with us."

It was odd suddenly, him in the doorway, standing between me and the work. Said it wasn't for me—no peace in sitting idly—but if he didn't mind, I'd like to see it through. He said, "Uh, sure," and, "We'll be back early in the afternoon," then they filed through the front door to their sedan, engine turned over twice before it caught. Through the thin curtain on their front window, I watched them head down the street, a right at the avenue. I was alone with the new tiles, the adhesive, the grout. And I got to laying them, working at my own pace, free of narrating the instructions. I sipped a beer while placing the tiles together, carefully, using all of my shoulders, all of my weight to set them faster. I applied the grout, smoothed it over, stepped lightly on them, bent at the waist to see if any of the ends had come up. When I finished, I checked the paint, sanded down some imperfections. I was alone in their home, all the lamps off, tall sun pitching through the window, and there were no signs of the fire. The history of that short burn had been erased. I walked the rest of the materials back to my garage, then my tools, locked their door behind me.

I'd appreciated so little of my home that week. Standing in my living room, I ran my hand along the edge of the bookshelf, rubbed the thin dust between the pads of my fingers. This was a good thing. I did this good thing. My legs ached, and I was about to sit down when there was a knock—Mrs. Cotton—and she smiled, relief flowing in the wrinkles around her eyes. She said, "Jude it's just so beautiful. We can't thank you enough."

Over her right shoulder, Mr. Cotton ushered the boys into their house and they waved from across the yard, disappearing past their threshold. When I turned back to her, she was holding a piece of paper to me. "The congregation got together and *passed the plate*, so to speak. They wanted to take the burden off of you. Off of us."

The check was signed by Pastor Mills. It didn't feel right. Not the church paying it, but the debt itself, didn't sit well with me anymore. Told her it was fine, I didn't want it. And her face changed, lit up with blood, pulled down at the seams. I said, "It's no burden."

She shook the check, the ends flapping. "Jude, we owe you this."

I didn't need them to pay it, didn't need the compensation. Said, "That's not why I did it. I don't want you to owe me anything."

She exhaled, the check pinched between her nails. I could tell that slip had, for her, a weight, and she just wanted to be free of it. I raised my hands up like surrender, and she started to put the check in my palm, but I made a fist, so she crumpled it, pushed the watermarked page into the gap between my thumb and curled fingers, my skin still white from the grout. She said, "We're always going to be owing. Please just take it."

It stuck to my dirty palm, and she turned back to her home. I couldn't watch her leave. When I knew she was gone, I went inside and shut my door, sat in my chair, looked at the amount, just as I quoted it, matched my ledger to the penny. I couldn't hear any of the street noise—no kids playing, no bugs in the woods, no cars in the road, just an autumn breeze brushing past. I went to the front window, and the neighborhood was still, sky gray, the leaves on the trees not bending but swaying just so, a blur, stroked by the wind, looked to me like a painting. I put the check down and took up the bottle, twisted out the cork and sipped it. The scotch tasted of smoke and cedar, and I pulled from it longer, swallowed twice, three times. The liquor slid down my throat, dragging a burn as it went. The char, the wood, the cinnamon made a furnace of my stomach. I set the bottle back and closed my eyes, focused on that peat flavor hot in me until it, too, boiled up and was gone. In its place, I felt a quickening—something quiet, patient, small and akin to grief, growing in the shadow of this good deed. I had no name for it just then, but in the order of my home, in the stillness of its embrace, I came to know it as reverence.

᠊᠊᠊

Brotherhood

Was told it meant support like sustenance—twin bed soldiers of one body. My older brother had a voice like knuckles, always spoke to me in bruises. I lived to argue. His front teeth crossed like hands holding, and I used to imagine loosing them down his throat. Too-fat kid that festered in his skin; I knew it was hard to be him based on how ashamed I was of his company. That's not to say he didn't teach me to throw a punch.

That snow day, the neighborhood jumped from playground to blizzard drift. My brother leapt and our neighbor, Stephen, cried *Avalanche!* I stood above, waiting for my turn to fall while they threw fists like generalizations—glancing, yet on the whole, inaccurate. My older brother, doe-legged with exhaustion, tripped, rolling on his back while Stephen booted the earth by his uncapped head.

Against the snow, his curls were my grandma's curls, his asymmetrical dimple, my mother's, and my blood tipped with the very violence he'd warmed in me. I'd grown up watching pain mark his face with pocks, yet to intervene meant denying the chance for a kick, not too wounding but hard enough to possibly drain the fury from him. While I lingered, they went home the way boys often do—full of hurt and unscathed.

The cold soaked my boots still frozen to the ledge. From the swing, my younger brother watched me hover, the noise in the chain singing—*Cow-ard. Weak-ling. Cow-ard. Weak-ling.*

⤶

I Want to Be This to Your That

When Sloane came to Baltimore, we saw that poetry reading with my friends—the reader all slumped into the microphone, his hand stuffed in a corduroy pocket, read that line *I want to be the Michael Jordan of your W4 form*. My friends and I got busy chewing it around, but she sped out a laugh, a cackle, singular, *HA*, and the room erupted around her. As the noise churned around me, I decided to get over my worry, to get over my preconceived notions on how this night might play out because there was something just so charming about her barbs: the way she talked like a valley girl but graduated with honors from NYU, the way she knew more about avant garde French cinema and Korean pop than anyone should, how she resembled a mermaid with all the wavy walnut hair and hourglass torso, that pouty look that says, "Follow me under." My friends and I were taking ourselves so seriously, worried about how our reactions might reflect on our lit journal, our adjunct jobs, and she heard the words—really just *heard* them. Her eyes refracted light from the yellow stage bulbs, and at the other end of them, I startled. So when we broke off and played Connect Four in that dingy little bar, and she asked if it was good to see her again, I meant it when I said, "I imagine this is how junkies feel when they're hocking a microwave or their mom's jewelry."

Sloane said, "That's so poignant. *So* romantic."

Later, in the back of that cab heading downtown to see her friend's band play, she put the knuckles of her spindly hand on my cheek—just put them there—as if she were taking my temperature. Each time the driver hit a pothole, the hips of our jeans rubbed. I knew she was still living with Mark, so I made like I was ignoring it. I hung out beside the stage, recognizing catchy songs that the band had played a couple of years earlier, when Sloane and I first dated. I'd met her at a show like this—twangy guitars over a strict beat, the singer doing his best Julian Casablancas. I didn't think when she asked to crash on my couch she'd meant she wanted me to sleep with her on it. As we came through the door, she said, "No sex or anything. Let's, like, watch a movie and pass out."

I told her my bed was more comfortable, but she dropped her bag against the coffee table and stretched her legs out on the chaise. She was a little tall for me in moments of nearness—when she tipped her head to my shoulder, it took us a while to get adjusted. With her hand on my navel, I asked, "What would Mark think?" And she didn't say anything, not another word, before she fell asleep. An infomercial prattling on the TV, her chest raised against that threadbare crewneck—I realized, of all the nights we shared sleep, I was always the first to drift off. Used to wait for her to come back from the bathroom, spearmint toothpaste on her breath. If we'd been drinking, she'd crack the window and smoke in bed, ashing her cigarettes in a porcelain teacup on the nightstand. Our relationship survived only that winter. The naked air stole the heat from under her covers, and when I woke back then, I wondering how long she'd been up, whether she minded how I'd left her alone.

~

Next morning, over coffee and a crick in my neck, she downplayed the contact, told me it was just a habit that she shouldn't have let herself slip back into. Yet, when I was dropping her off for the train to DC so she could follow that band for the next night of their DMV tour, she begged me to come with her. I knew she had plans to meet up with Alby, whom she was still referring to as the man of her dreams. He, the grown up, late thirties, goth Superman, straight-fucking-edge, horror movie connoisseur, and me, the guy she once referred to as halfway between her high school boyfriend and the man she will one day marry.

"No. God no," I said. "Where would I even sleep?"

"We'll find you a place. Worst case: Alby's sofa."

I leaned over the edge of the platform, checking for the train.

"Olivia will be there," Sloane said. "She *looks* like she could be my older sister."

"So?"

"You wouldn't want to fuck my older sister?"

But I didn't want to be so cheap anymore. I wanted to do things that I couldn't drink myself away from, that I wouldn't just laugh off later. No longer that guy who would sleep with your sister, your best friend, the guy who chewed straight through your story of unrequited love into the bed sheets of the girl you pined for. I was tired of losing friends, of disregarding my nights. I was finally over flings. I got on the train only because she said, in her exasperated way, "Who am I going to hang out with before the show? Keep me company. At least until then."

We got off the Metro in Columbia Heights, started drinking at two. We stopped at bars that she used to frequent before moving to New York, a little story for each one: This is where I met Dan, that DJ kid. He spit in my mouth once. I used to hang out with Felix, here. You remember him? He was the one who kept trying to get me to move back to LA. I found out he was sleeping with Tina the whole time we dated. This was me and Thad's spot. I know you know Thad.

I said, "We broke up because you had a thing for Thad."

"Broke up? We weren't dating."

I made that hand puppet of a bird's mouth, opening and closing. It was the distance, she'd argued—that we couldn't function being an hour apart. She said I should've moved to DC, to her, and I replied that I thought we *weren't dating*. She got all quiet then, and we agreed to slow down. We'd drank our way to dinner and were in rough shape, and I was looking at the scuffed brass knob at the end of the bar, wondering what I was shielding from these stories, the details that out of anyone else's mouth would have been funny and not off-putting. I said, "What makes you think I want to know any of this?"

"I like these sorts of things. Ex-sex-tapestries. I know you have some."

And I did. But there was no humor in fleshing them out, not with her. I kept picturing the late-night texts Thad sent while we were lying in bed, the calls that interrupted our dinners, growing the roots for the fight that Sloane and I had right before I spent a weekend in the bed of a mutual friend. We didn't hang out for two years, had only started texting again last month. A block from the venue, she wrapped her index finger around the bell of my wrist, brought my hand around her waist.

The walls of the club were black, the stage, black, the bar, black. I paid five dollars for a Budweiser and the band played the same set. We stood in a group of Sloane's friends, and she kept looking toward the door to see when Alby would arrive, talked about him with everyone but me. Her friends were an attractive collection of the DC lifestyle I'd come to know—days of high-stress jobs following late night excess-driven relief. There was a party at Olivia's after, and she said Alby got delayed, was going to meet her there. It was late, about eleven, and I set an alarm for midnight so that I wouldn't miss the last train back north to Baltimore. She kept saying, "Just stay, just stay," and then stared at her phone, texting him with her left hand, rocks glass dangling in her right. When her friends congested at the exit of the club, Sloane held her hand out, expecting mine.

Olivia taught English at a private high school and did look quite like Sloane, but older, handsomely weathered, her brown hair dull in the curls and her smile lines pointing fingers toward her eyes. In another life, if I'd met her first, I would have pursued her—that itch in the pit of my stomach to know her better—but I could tell a mutual friend, Jonah, liked her, and I didn't want to be that guy anymore, to be an intruder. And Olivia joked that Jonah and I looked alike as well—ambiguously Asian, raw denim, flannel shirts. She made a joke that the four of us were some sort of Murakami universe mirror paradigm. It was a pleasant surprise, her bringing up Murakami, and we talked about *Wind-up Birds* and *Sputnik Sweethearts* until Olivia nudged me, dropped her voice, said, "You see those two guys over there? Don't look. Okay now, look now."

I half-turned, half-turned back. She said a couple months ago, they had a really awkward threesome with her roommate. Before I could picture it, before I could ask what an awkward threesome entailed, Sloane turned to us, made a triangle out of our grouping and said, "Phil really wants a threesome. He says it's the last box he needs to fill in sex-fantasy-bingo." Something I'd told her years ago in confidence. Something I no longer cared about.

Olivia laughed. "Last box, huh?"

Sloane slid her phone from her pocket, shot me a look, left me to wade in the pause. I was never one for blushing, but Olivia just bopped to the music, said, "Have you ever noticed how some authors find a way to work anal sex into a narrative? For absolutely no reason."

"Like Murakami." I inflected.

"And Franzen."

"Who else? Maybe Lawrence?"

She squinted, considering this, said, "It's like they're inviting you to mine what you want from it. Which is lazy, right? Acting like there's some special meaning to be deciphered."

I could be instinctively contrary when drinking, got a lot of pleasure out of playful arguing. Asked her what she would think if it wasn't symbolism—why does everything have to be twinned, a conduit or reflection? What if it was just the act, what if that was the point. She shrugged, said that meaning *is* worth, right? It's what cleaves a melody from all the noise. You put two things together, and it might just stay those two things—completely forgettable—but sometimes that nearness creates, chemically, something near unsayable. Like harmony but not that simple. Those were the things worth discussing, worth clutching.

It wasn't a new idea to me, but hearing it spring from her mouth grabbed me by the ankles, set me stiff and sobered. They told me to lean in and stoke the conversation, but before I could, Sloane came back, a little loose on her kitten heels but graceful in her stupor, almost a dancer, except for the handful of errant hairs pulled and powdered through the foundation on her cheeks, now darkened and stained by a swell of tears. She sucked air in through hiccups, took Olivia's hand and headed for the bedroom. I followed the scraps of choked words that came bubbling over her hysteria.

Olivia held Sloane's hand as she crumbled to the floor at the foot of the bed, one heel popping off in the movement. I leaned on the doorframe, adjusted the fold of my cuff. From what I deciphered in their clumsy and cyclical conversation, Alby had thought Sloane was going to wait at the venue so they could walk over together—didn't want to make the trek alone—and Sloane was upset that he was now going to a dance party that his friend was hosting instead.

"He was so nasty to me," she said. The mascara running down her cheeks reminded me of the cave paintings I'd seen in a coffee table book. She splayed her legs in a *V* and Olivia sat on the foot of the bed, unknotting her hair. "He kept calling me *fucking stupid.*"

Olivia told Sloane not to deal with it, just ignore him for a while, but Sloane said she had basically come on this trip to see him, said, "Why is he so nasty?" The cycle repeated, Olivia reiterating in different words, and Sloane defending, bemoaned at the idea that she might not see him tonight, and eventually, my legs got tired, and I wanted to feel closer, so I sat down between Sloane's feet while she admitted she might love him. Her jaw buckled around the word.

I said, "You shouldn't be so caught up."

Olivia gave a nod. Jonah peeked his head in the doorway, saw the tears brimming in Sloane's eyes and ducked out.

Sloane said, "God, I must look like a child."

The alarm on my phone went off. Someone changed the music in the living room from Missy Elliott to Smashing Pumpkins, shouted "Throwback!" I brushed threads of carpet from my jeans. The alarm on my phone sounded again, and Sloane told me to stay but I didn't want to console her, didn't want to be there for her like that, to have to wait for everyone to stop drinking so I could fall asleep on the couch. Olivia offered her roommate's bed, said she wasn't coming back tonight. That look of Sloane's, the widening of the eyes, the neediness—and I wanted to be needed—so I sat down again, but she didn't reward me with a smile.

Olivia gathered Sloane's curls behind her shoulders. She said, "No need to waste the night," then touched my scalp with her palm as she passed into the body of the apartment. Even if I left now, I wouldn't make the last train. I sipped my beer, watched Sloane pick the mint nail polish off the back of her thumb, asked her why she was still with Mark. She slipped her other heel off and closed the *V* of her legs so that the bulbs of her ankles touched the hems of my jeans. She pulled the wet label off her beer and crumpled it up in her palm. "I want a hundred different things, depending on the day. It's just how I am."

We'd gone drink for drink all night. She surrendered the bottom of her beer to me, and I called her a loser. When I bent the neck of the bottle to my lips, she nudged me over with her foot. Half of me was adrift alongside her, the other wanted to be where she landed. I stood and offered her my hand, and she said, "My phone's dead, anyway."

In the living room, a handful of people were scattered around the coffee table and Jonah led them in a singing of *Tonight, Tonight*. We smoked cigarettes with Olivia by the window, one per song. Sloane looked through the panes, eyes searching the street. I conjoined my shoulder to hers, did my whiniest Billy Corgan impression—howling, "Despite of my rage," snarling, "You know I'm not dead," even took a few laughs from her. Later, Jonah passed out on the sofa, and Olivia told Sloane they could split her bed.

The other bedroom was a glorified closet off the kitchen, an alcove with a sliding pantry door barely big enough for its twin bed and dresser topped with a box fan. I folded my button down beside it, placed my cellphone and keys and wallet underneath. I went to the bathroom to take a piss and when I came back, Sloane stood in the doorway, her heels dangling from her fingers. She said, "Let's go to bed."

From the kitchen, I could see Jonah's feet on the armrest—one shoe on, one shoe off. Sloane sat down by the pillows, pulled off her sweater and undid her jeans, then lay on her back where the twin bed met the wall. If I listened carefully, I could hear my lungs bellowing, not pleading but suggesting, telling me *Sleep on the floor. Sleep on the chair. Sleep anywhere.* But the beer in my stomach was loud, too, and I wanted the warmth of flesh to my flesh, I wanted to put an arm over her. I wanted. And I took off my socks and balled them in my oxfords and lay down beside her. Though someone had rolled down the volume, the Smashing Pumpkins playlist repeated.

We were on top of the covers. I faced the ceiling, one arm behind my head, listening to my heart beat against my inner ear— from elbow to shoulder, the only parts of us touching. The apartment was loud, but consistently so, and I turned on my side toward her, placed my arm across her belly and started to nod off. And then *Tonight, Tonight* was playing again, and her breath in my mouth woke me, the cold tip of her nose touching the divot in my upper lip. I could taste the sourness of the beer she'd drank that night, could smell her face wash, and with no pretense of being asleep, we pressed our lips together. We hadn't had sex in years, but sliding down the bed so our faces met, skinning her shirt over all that hair, inhaling the crevice between her collarbones was remembering. I put my fingers along the curves of her ribs, and after a time she turned and pulled her hair beneath her so that the nape of her neck was on my mouth. My right arm was trapped. I grazed her navel with my knuckles, and she wiggled her jeans past the crest of her hips. When I strummed the elastic of her underwear, she said, "We shouldn't."

Billy Corgan was telling us that God is empty and she took my left hand by the wrist, guiding it. I recalled how to touch her like one suddenly knows a secret handshake with an old friend. We moved together, swaying, shifting, and slowly her jeans drew down as she rubbed her calves together, clutching my belt loop, clutching me to her, and then we were trading some inner sentiments for that mutual difficulty. Or maybe I was lying to myself, maybe it was easy. It wasn't the right thing to do, but the wrongness of it was satiating—that hunger teased up and fed. She pulled me from her before either of us finished and held me, wet and flagging.

～

When I woke in the morning, we were laying spine to spine, my knees dangling over the floor and hers wedged to the wall. Sunlight underlined the bottom of the folding door. I put my shoulder blades to the mattress and she took my wrist in her hand. My jeans were still undone.

I said, "I feel like trash."

"Yeah. This hangover is going to be great."

Jonah was shoeless, and in the room past the couch, Olivia, too, hadn't stirred. There was a slowness to it—them asleep together, separated by the wall—their attraction unfulfilled yet somehow still breathing, and I was envious of their patience, their satisfaction. I only knew how to be eager. Sloane walked me to coffee, then to the Metro. She said, "We should just pretend that didn't happen."

I adjusted the cup in my hand.

"Or like, I don't know. Post-date it. Let's act like it happened sometime before."

I said, "It doesn't work like that."

She dug through her purse for her birth control, freed it, swallowed. I clicked my tongue. A chill hung in the morning air. The row houses crept closer to the road with each block toward the station. Then we were at a cross street and the tenements gave way to businesses. For a time, we were alone. The elbows of my shirt-sleeves were slick, the knees of my jeans loose. She shouldered her bag. "That's how it has to be."

As we approached the corner, I stepped around a light post onto the curb. She walked along the glass of a storefront. A pharmacy, then a McDonalds, then an H&R Block. Her heels scuffed the cement with each step, and I had to lengthen my gait to keep up.

"So it didn't mean anything?"

"Of course it did. But Phil," she dragged a finger along the window, "it didn't happen."

The repetition of the words annoyed me. I let some coffee settle under my tongue, jutting my jaw. We came to the escalator that descended beneath the street to the Metro station. I told her I'd just talk to her later. We embraced and she pressed an arm around me. I let her go and turned. She said my name again, squeezed my ribs, brought me to her, and I felt limp in her grasp, waiting for her hands to fall away. She said, "Be good to yourself," then stood at the mouth of the station as I descended on the escalator. While I put money on my fare card, I pictured how long she stayed there, whether she turned when I was out of view, or if she needed something to happen, some interruption to signal the end of the moment.

On the train, the rails underneath the car did not pass with a *clack* but hummed electronically into my ear as I rested my head against the metal wall. I brought my feet closer, rubbing the soles of my shoes against the carpet. The rubber cushion crunched under the weight of my hips. Yet I could feel no depth to me. The train stopped and a few passengers got on, a few off. And maybe I could well something up in me again. Maybe I could get some of it back, some meaning, if I abandoned even a little bit of my want. The train whirred in my ear and moved through a tunnel, dimming the car, then emerged in a ravine between two boroughs heading north. If I could learn to wait, to learn to move slow, and if not slow, then not at all—maybe I could change into something gathered and cultivated, organized even, constructed and sturdy, capable of withholding some toppling, some mess. The fluorescent lights flickered and sustained. I whispered a wish to be more than fevered flesh, more than cold sweat, a history of shivers, of covers pulled, the culmination of friction, and listened, waited, swayed to the shifting in the line.

I have learned how to move. Teach me to be still.

Fontanelle

Summer before I went to college, I worked at a scrapyard tucked along that stretch of 270 where the cars come screaming past Gaithersburg, fleeing DC's endless rush hour. I was a spot-filler, helping different sections when they were short-staffed. This meant stripping industrial cables for copper or hosing down the half-mile track of dirt road that circled the administrative building, wetting the dust to keep it from billowing up as the trucks came through.

The day I met you was my last shift. Since dawn, I'd been stationed on the aluminum compactor, dumping cans onto the conveyor belt until the trap was full, and Sweet closed the gate and threw the switch. We stood there, tan arms folded, watching the piston drive the plate into the body of the machine, the crackle of aluminum compressing before the catch hissed and the flattened metal emptied into a shipping container. Sweet usually helped me level out the refuse, but his Nextel was chirping, so he flipped it open and whispered. That's how I knew he was talking to his girlfriend—the low tones. Last batch had been three bins of ancient Coors Banquet cans stained tobacco brown at the rim. I was used to pinching my nose while I pushed the discs deeper into the container—the saccharin odor of soda and liquor turned my stomach—but these had been rinsed out, the only smell being that same toxic rust that perfumed from the stacks of junk metal.

Sweet kicked at the gravel with the toe of his boot. He had his hand tucked into his armpit, a smile upturning his black mustache. When I'd started working there a couple months earlier, he'd told me he was "dumb in love." I wasn't sure how to take that, whether he meant being in a relationship made him stupid or if he was simply not good with women. He'd moved from El Salvador a few years earlier, and his accent was thick in the vowels. He said he'd gotten his nickname because he used to be a junior Olympic boxer—that he'd mastered the sweet science—but I figured it was from the lightness of his tone, how he never said a word that didn't sound cheerful. That alone made him difficult to read—couldn't tell if he was being ironic, sarcastic, sincere.

I understood, now, that he meant "dumb in love" to mean he pushed his common sense aside at the first word of his girlfriend, like when I was coming off the ladder, and he was talking on his phone—a code of conduct violation. Three of those and you were fired, no pleas, no mercy. Sweet knew I'd play lookout. I'd only gotten the job because my mom was still going to church. Half the managerial staff was in the priesthood, and even though I hadn't attended in years, they hired me as a favor. The men in the yard didn't trust my company, thought I might be spying for management, wouldn't exchange anything except gruff nods on their way into the fields. They could tell I wouldn't be here for any real length. Sweet wasn't cold to me. And he knew I was grateful that he let me follow him around, that he showed me how to make it through a day.

Sweet shut his phone, adjusted the fit of his cap, showing the sweat-cleaned skin the brim had protected from the yard's grime. I grabbed another bin of those vintage Coors cans, lifted one out to inspect it. I said, "You think these could be worth something?"

"As what, a collector's item?" He let out a cackle and punched me on the shoulder as he grabbed the next bin. "Come on, 'rillo, cans are all peddlers. People just trying to find a few dollars in their junk." We hefted the bins, the maroon and navy script blurring as the aluminum spilled onto the conveyer. When we went for the next load, he reconsidered, said, "Though, if anyone found some money in all this trash, it would be you."

The yard's business focused on bulk shipments, picking up a semi's worth of unsorted scrap metal and refining it for sale. But, along the south end of the admin building, near the front gate, there was a row of scales for walk-ups. Junkers and contractors could bring radiators pulled from dumpsters or piping leftover from a build, and we'd trade it for cash. This was the year before bright copper skyrocketed from one-fifty a pound to three times that, right before copper theft from construction sites became an epidemic. Sweet ran the scales because, as our boss, Arnie, said, "He can speak well and knows how not to get ripped off." Arnie was the head bursar, balanced the sales tickets at the end of the day, running the tellers who sat behind the windows, punching timecards and exchanging receipts.

At lunch, Sweet went with the forklift drivers to a bodega down the way. Arnie let me eat in his office so that he could try and convert me back to Mormonism. We'd eat with our hardhats in our laps, talking about work, then he'd bend the conversation to all the events for youth going on at the ward. That day, he'd asked if I wanted to join their intermural basketball league playing against other church teams in the area. I'd enjoyed it when I was younger but didn't miss the hours I'd spent in seminary, in Sunday school. I had no nostalgia for the gospel.

We worked seven-to-three shifts, so lunch ran before eleven. A lot of the guys didn't eat that early, choosing instead to smoke cigarettes and drink cups of sugared coffee on the ramp to the main garage. Past the cable stripper and the rows of upturned spools, Uncle Tad had his confection stand. Today, Tad is probably dead. He was old back then—seventy or seventy-five. He managed the worker supplies, everything but hardhats. If you needed a new pair of gloves, you brought your old ones to Tad and exchanged them. But if you lost something or forgot it at home, you couldn't get a replacement without being reprimanded. Tad called them demerits, you either owed the lost item or had to pay the list price, otherwise supplies were closed to you. I'd seen guys driving fork-lifts through the stacks of twisted steel signage with no masks, breathing in the dust kicked up by the wheels. This exile included Tad's side business selling dollar coffee and Little Debbies for a quarter. Arnie told me that the yard funded it all, they just let Tad think it was his. Tad wasn't all there, so to speak. He was a mem-ber of the ward, so Arnie found work for him. They said the empowerment was good for his state of mind.

Sweet lost shit all the time—a glove in the parking lot, a mask on his way to the bathroom. Told me shifts were easier if you had a routine, to keep you focused. He said, "This work is mindless. It's too easy to go somewhere else in your head." He beat an unmatched glove against his thigh. "So, you leave yourself moments to look forward to, those little things throughout the day that aren't so bad, and just focus on that plan. When you don't have a plan, you lose shit."

My routine featured an ice cream bar after lunch, then a cup of coffee with cream, the burnt roast swirling with the aftertaste of the sugar. Sometimes, when I drink cheap coffee, I remember how standing in the middle of all that refuse made it impossible to pic-ture the world moving beyond the property fence. And there was relief in that seclusion.

My girlfriend and I had broken up just before the summer began. She was off to Elon, and I was going to Scranton to live at my grandfather's and start college—major undecided. At the start of the summer, we'd sat in the parking lot outside my mom's apartment, throats raw from arguing. She kept saying, "What's the point?" I got out of her car and climbed the fire escape to my bedroom window. Now, at work, I left my cellphone in the glove box of my '86 Corolla, didn't have to worry about missing mes-sages from anyone. We'd dated since sophomore year, and that change seemed, at first, indigestible. In the beginning of August, as I crumpled the paper cup in my fist and dropped it into the trash, I was relieved to be free of our rhythm— how she'd reveal all the nasty things her parents said about me, then bickering, a make-up handjob.

"To the scales, *'rillo*," Sweet said. I followed him through the piles of steel appliances that the crane operators sorted between the garage and the admin building. The sun hit the glass of an oven door, threw glare into my safety goggles. Sweet kept looking at text messages on his phone, singing that McDonald's jingle— *ba da da da dahhh, I'm loving it*. He said, "Life is strange, huh? Sometimes you're stuck in the mud. Then a little heat frees you." He punctuated himself with a wink. I'd been too young to be anything but wordless when the conversation hinted at sex, so I adjusted the strap on my hardhat and refit it over my hair.

It was pay-Friday, at three we lined up at the teller windows to cash out. In the crowd with other workers, Sweet spoke Spanish, and I stood behind him, not too close to appear desperate for attention. The yard was paying me under the table with cash from the scale clerks. Depending on the day, I might get a stack of fives and tens instead of big bills. The other men checked their hours against their punch cards. One man said something to the circle of us, nodding at the cash I'd been counting. When the laughter died down, Sweet gestured at my envelope, told me that I needed to get my papers.

I waited for Sweet to grab his things from his locker, the other men filing out past me into the parking lot. He emerged from the backroom rolling curses under his breath, said he'd hoped his other glove would be in his bag. "What's five more dollars for Tad, right?"

I handed him my pair, told him I had backups at home. He asked if I was sure, and I waved him off, said of course. We walked out through the front gate, the security guard closing it behind us. The end of work reminded me of the afternoons school let out—the way the men blasted music through open car windows, peeling out of the parking lot and up the narrow strip of road to the highway. That feeling of being uncaged, of racing into the moments of freedom that were already ticking away toward the next morning's shift even as you buckled your seatbelt and started home—I spent this time alone. When my friends texted, I didn't answer, unwilling to discuss the breakup, my new job. I wanted to make some money and move as quickly as possible. And I did, and we lost touch, and I could never really exert enough effort to get them back. That was the summer when I became obsessed with Blockbuster's DVD mailer program, watching movies until I fell asleep. I was comfortable at home, my mother locked in her office on conference calls. If she or I didn't make dinner, I'd grab a sub from the corner market and eat it on the fire escape, watching the sun go down between the two high rises across the way, sinking into a canopy of trees. The bruised orange light flooded the branches, didn't quite mask the cable-linked towers leading to the electric substation.

Sweet and I had just cleared the property fence that first time I saw you, clutched to your mother's chest as she shut her Volvo door. I didn't see you at first, distracted by Lane's features—they've always been startling in their sharpness—cheekbones cutting a triangle to her chin. You were just a little spot of bare skin puddled in cloth, barely old enough to support the weight of your head. Lane looked around the lot, not expectantly, just tucking her limp black hair behind her ear and heading toward the yard.

Sweet folded his three gloves in the back pocket of his jeans, asked her if she needed help. She looked past me, toward the gate. A thin layer of sweat coated her pale skin. She said, "Maybe. I— uh. I need to buy something back."

I came alongside Sweet, saying, "You'll have to come tomorrow. We're closed."

"Have some manners, *'rillo*." Sweet nudged my hardhat with his fist, knocking the sun flap over my eyes. I wanted to push him back but realized that this sort of physicality was improper, suddenly aware of how you occupied the gap between us, a pale face swaddled in a paisley scarf. He said, "What is it you needed back?"

She brought her purse to her hip, produced a manila envelope and receipt. She said she'd sold some scrap yesterday, but she shouldn't have. It wasn't hers to sell. Sweet told her there might still be a manager in the office, turning to me, his moustache fingering over his lips. The way he prodded me with his eyes, I knew he wanted me to run and check, but I was annoyed with him for the previous emasculating shove. When I didn't offer, Sweet said, "I'll go find out."

I turned to watch him plod down the gravel parking lot to the fence, knocking on the security window. Shoulder-to-shoulder with Lane, I was too uncomfortable to make eye contact, unsure how to be in her presence, the presence of a baby. I looked at the toes of my boots, water-stained and scuffed. I said, "What'd you sell?"

Her voice was underlined by an eagerness that she suppressed, saying, "I came by in the morning with a bunch of beer cans. Really old ones."

I said, "They're probably in the refinery by now."

"All of them?"

When I didn't speak, she exhaled, her shoulders sagging. I said I was sorry, then turned toward my Corolla a ways off in the lot, waiting for Sweet to return before I left as a matter of politeness. When I turned back, Lane was facing me, and I could see you for the first time, button nose and blue eyes. You looked too clean and white for the gravel, the dirt, and roughness that bordered us. She said your name was Carl, an old name, but it belonged to your father. There was a warmth in my throat as your toothless mouth curled into a smile, your hands reaching for her hair. She asked if my name was "*'rillo*," and I laughed. Told her it's short for *amarillo*—yellow.

"Your name is Yellow?"

"It's an Asian joke. My father is Chinese."

"Is that it? I couldn't place it." She bounced you in her arms as she spoke, said, "It's a handsome combination."

The tall sun leaned toward the highway. Beyond the fence, the occasional rattle of metal against metal sounded as the cranes sorted into the evening. Pillars of smoke rose out of the furnace stacks. I didn't feel the gravity of my home pulling me, no urge to rush back to my routine of movies and a full night's sleep. We waited for Sweet to get back, made small talk. Lane lived north in Frederick where she worked remotely for a web design firm. The longer we spoke, the more aware of our eight-year age difference I became, and I wanted, suddenly, to be where she was, grounded in something certain. A career job. A child. Sweet emerged from the fence, and as he approached, she looked up from you, seemed to reconsider me for a moment. "Let me give you my number, in case something turns up."

Told her my cell was in my car, but I copied her phone number onto a dollar bill and folded it in my fist. I knew that by tomorrow's shift, there wouldn't be anything left to return, but it felt easier to relent in this moment. When Sweet was within talking distance, he said, "Arnie closed the tills for the day. I'm sorry. We open at seven-thirty tomorrow."

Lane said, "Well, what I was looking for might already be gone, apparently. Thank you for checking."

Sweet lifted the brim of his hat, said it was nothing. When she was in her Volvo and heading to the through-way, Sweet stuck his chin toward the dollar I'd folded in my hand, said, "You got her number, *'rillo*?"

"She brought all those beer cans. I said I'd let her know if any were left."

He scoffed and started up the lot toward his Tercel. My car was on the way to his, and I asked what was up. His black hair curled under the snapback of his cap, lifting as he shrugged his shoulders. He said, "You really going to call her if we find some of those shit beer cans? Or did you just want her number?"

"She gave it to me. I didn't ask."

He passed in front of my Corolla, picked at the broken plastic of the headlight with his middle finger. "I saw how you looked at her, *'rillo*," he said, his voice low, thawing with concern. "She's pretty, sure. But she's got a kid. You really want to get involved with that?"

I opened my car door, tossed my hardhat into the passenger seat. I said it wasn't like that, it was just a nicety, to put her at ease. I said, "What should I have done, told her that I compacted all of her shit this morning? Told her not to get her hopes up?"

"That would have been kinder."

My window rattled as I shut the door. Sitting there, Sweet framed by the windshield ahead of me, I couldn't recall, exactly, Lane's face, but I remembered the itch I felt as I skimmed the angles of her profile, the soft crook in her nose, the bower of her clavicle. There was a certain grace to the way she held you, a confidence in the striped muscle of her forearm, gripping you to her. Sweet knocked on my window, and I waited a moment before I cranked it down. He put his arm on the doorframe, held himself up as he bent at the waist, head level with mine.

He told me a story about growing up after his father died of a poor heart. Sweet was ten, and a year later, his mother got this boyfriend who was young, maybe mid-twenties. He helped out with the bills, sure, but he was still wild with youth—came over late at night on the weekends, banging on the door. One morning, Sweet was brushing his teeth, and the boyfriend came into the bathroom, stinking of *guaro*, and relieved himself in the toilet. Sweet said, "I look over at him, give him this look like *Hey, I'm in here, can't you wait?* and this fool asks me if I'm trying to peek at his junk. I just want him to leave so I can get ready for church, and I don't know, I guess since he mentioned it, I looked down. I was just a kid. I didn't know how to handle myself. He's holding his junk, and, I mean—I don't know if it's cause I was so little back then, but it looked fucking huge." His face contorted into a sneer. Laughing once, he said, "Biggest dick I've ever seen. To this day. It was gross. Then he shakes it once and tells me to take a good look. He says I'll never be *that* much of a man."

For a moment, neither of us spoke, and I became aware of the sweat and dirt caked into the ditches of my elbows, the back of my neck. Sweet said, "I'm telling you, *'rillo*. I think about that shit every day."

"I'm not that kind of person."

Sweet pushed off the doorframe, stood next to the car, his shadow cast across the hood. He spoke slower, said, "You'd be that. Maybe some other way, but you would still be just that. It's too hard to make family, you know? I mean, it's too hard to *become* someone's family. Think about it."

"I'll see you Monday."

"Do me a favor, okay? Spend that dollar."

The gravel crunched under his boots as he walked off. I started my car and rolled through the lot, my tires kicking up a pallid dust that lapped at my open window. As I moved past him, Sweet called out, "Hey, *'rillo, 'rillo!*" holding the gloves above his head. From my driver's seat, the folds of plastic-coated cloth blocked the sun, turned him to a silhouette in the shape of a wave, a goodbye. He said, "Listen, I wasn't trying to scold you. I'm just trying to look out for you, man."

"It's okay. Don't worry about it. I'll see you Monday."

"Sure, sure. *Cuidado, hombre.*" He let his arm drop—the falling hand struck his thigh with a clap. "Take care."

∼

Lane named you Carl after your father, but since she kicked him out, she liked to think of it in the context of the dad in *Family*

Matters, that she'd always admired how he wanted ease but couldn't bring himself to admit Urkel's accidents gave his life an unfamiliar purpose. She said that's what she wanted for you—a certain excitement, an attention, even if you are unwilling to greet it. She said, "I just don't want him to be alone."

This was halfway through my second Guinness in that bar across the tracks in Old Towne, the one with the Christmas bulbs hung from the gutter, half burnt out and faded piss-yellow. I'd been only two blocks from the scrapyard before I texted her, and she said she was going to get an early dinner before she got back on the road, asked me if I wanted to join. We decided on that bar because it didn't card—Sweet took me there my first Friday, said I should celebrate surviving my week. Your mother got pastrami, said she had gotten hooked on it while she was pregnant. She lifted the bread from a pool of oil stained scarlet on the plate and shrugged, said, "I thought blood would be good for the baby."

Lane was smart in a way that made me feel, suddenly, like I was seeing life from the bottom of a well. When I showed up at the bar, I went to the bathroom and washed my face in the sink, cupping water in my hands and clearing the soot. The overhead light in our booth lit you stark white and poured shadows from the tops of Lane's cheekbones. She asked me what I was going to study at school and was gentle when I told her I didn't know. She always spoke to me in a tone that welcomed me even when it scolded, like she was trying to draw up the better version of me, and maybe that was why I believed, from this beginning, that your mother could do no wrong.

"Those cans were half shot with rust," I said. "Least you got some money for them."

"They weren't mine to sell."

Your father had collected them, and when she'd kicked him out a few months before, he couldn't find a place to store them while he looked for a new place to live. She told me they'd met when she was sixteen and started her bachelor's at UMD. He was much older—twice her age—taught classes in radio production and thought she was *so beautiful*. I said, "That didn't strike you as weird? I mean, you were a teenager."

"Well, how old are you now?" she said. "You're still a person, right?"

At eighteen, the dark beer was strange on my tongue, had to work to keep a straight face with every sip. Lane was good at teasing out any discomforts I kept hidden. She said, "I'm kidding. He had no way of knowing I wasn't *of age*. We were just friends at first. He was with someone until I was, like, twenty."

Over the years, I learned your father loved T. Rex and gas station fruit pies, the ones filled with jelly that come wrapped in wax paper. Lane said he was stick-thin, drawn out by cigarettes and years of heroin. From the pictures, I can see the roots of your complexion, your square brow. She never told me the reason for their break, but it had to do with his sobriety.

In the bar, she asked about my family, propping her chin on her fist. When she narrowed her eyes, I could feel myself losing grip on the aspects of my upbringing I refrained from talking about. Told her that my father had been a sheet metal mechanic for the Marines. In Vietnam, he patched helicopters, but spending his days on an island waiting for the birds to come back from combat was too boring for him, so he got moved to gunner. He was one of those men whose PTSD slipped through undiagnosed into the 90s. My mother was unhappy, and when he sensed it, his temper boiled over. They divorced when I was in elementary school.

Lane buoyed me along by offering sympathy—her hand, briefly, atop mine—asking questions about my wellbeing, and I wanted to be coddled in that way, thought that her compassion was a sign of her interest in me. I fed into it, said, "My dad was obsessed with video games. A week before I was born, he dragged my mom two hours to Philly to buy a Nintendo when it came out.

I'd gotten in the habit of avoiding him—playing outside, hanging out at friends' houses. I'd only ever get to play it when he was at work. So, when I was nine, I accidentally saved over his Zelda file. I don't know. It got out of control."

"Over a video game?"

"He had a lot of hours in it."

Our server cleared the plates. The happy hour crowd that had gathered at the bar thickened the room with noise. I ordered my third drink, and Lane got another serving of fries to split. She'd been rocking your carrier with her elbow. I'd almost forgotten you were there, so still in your half-sleep. I said, "Do you miss any of it? The freedom? Drinking?"

"Sure, sometimes," she smoothed her eyebrow with the pad of her thumb. "But don't change the subject—what happened?"

It's a funny thing, those memories we avoid retelling out of the fear that they can't be conveyed clearly, that there isn't enough time in a conversation to convince someone of the events while also reconstructing your own person in light of them. To say, this is something that happened to me, but I'm okay. I said, "He hardly ever hit me with a fist. It was just a lot of shoving, grabbing my shoulders. When he screamed, his voice cracked. It was such a hideous sound, now that I think about it. So, it wasn't anything special. He pushed me, and I fell into our coffee table. The way I landed, I broke my arm." I pointed to the spot below my elbow where the bone had fractured. I finished the dregs of my drink, and we split the check. "I think the three of us could sense it was over after that."

Lane said I shouldn't drive, asked me if I wanted to come back to her place and listen to some music. She used to rent a rowhome in the historic downtown part of Frederick. The lilac paint on the siding looked like velvet reflecting the honey-colored light from the streetlamps. For a couple hours, before she put you down for the night, we took turns dancing with you in the living room.

Lane played Joy Division, then the Strokes, and holding you to my chest, I slid in gentle circles on the hardwood. She said, "He loves the movement, it makes him giddy, and then he passes out." You had this dollop of chocolate hair on your crown, and when Lane held you, she cupped your head in her palm, covering it, saying, "I'm terrified of his soft spot. I'm not clumsy, but with my luck, I'd find a way to hit it." She was petting you, looking directly into your eyes now heavy with sleep. She said, "I'm always thinking about failing him."

As the song ended, her dance slowed to a stop. Lane's posture—her neck craned over you, her arms curled beneath the rounded corners of your body—was so gentle it looked severe in the muscles of her body. I knew that moment couldn't be unseen, and in the smallest way, I felt myself age. When the next track started, I stood behind her, looking over her shoulder at your face set in sleep. I put my hand on her back, got us swaying with the rhythm of the music.

I never told Lane that I hadn't had sex until that night, but I think, in my ineptness, she could tell. Lying in her bed after, naked but covered at the waist by her comforter, she said, "Do you feel any better?" then laughed, and I didn't understand the joke, but she held me around my ribs. I felt coveted. She strummed the hairs growing out of the scar on my forearm, and I told her that the worst thing about it was the men in my church knew my dad had done it, knew he was violent. All they did was shake their heads at my cast when they thought I couldn't see. Lane said, "Some men are weak."

I didn't feel any different having told her. In her bed, I realized that my hesitation was not about my own perception of strength—I didn't want people to vilify my father. We didn't leave her apartment that weekend. I left Monday morning to pick up my car so that I wouldn't get a ticket. I never went back to the scrapyard. She'd ask me to spend my last few weeks in Maryland with her, or maybe it had been my idea, wanting so helplessly to feel grounded. As I drove to my mother's to pick up more clothing, the hard hat in the passenger seat rattled with the bumps in the highway. For a moment, with the thin, warm air of that August morning drifting through the body of my car, I could hear Sweet singing a jingle under his breath as I followed him through the stacks of refuse, disappearing into that walled-off world in which I let life slip through me, unnoticed.

~

When I moved back from Pennsylvania, you were already talking. I'd just finished my associate's, and Lane was speaking with me again. She'd asked me not to be in touch, said our lives were both in transition and that made for the worst kind of relationship. But sometimes, over the course of those two years, after I drank a six-pack and the beer propelled me to risk her anger, I'd send her a message, and sometimes, in the morning, she would answer. I guess her resolve had worn thin once I got back home. When she answered the door—chambray slacks belted high on her waist, her blouse unbuttoned—there was something drawn-out to her that struck me, in my middle, as handsome. You were on her hip, wrapping your fists in her hair. The natural brown was showing in her roots, and with the early summer strangling the day with humidity, her grown-out bob clung to her neck. I didn't know if you recognized me, couldn't tell if your grin was particular to my company. She invited me in, and as I stood in her living room that was so much the same as the month I lived there except the pile of laundry on the ottoman and the toys littered across the hard-wood, she thrust you into my arms. Yours was a good weight. You liked to be held, were decisive in that, and while she put a pot of coffee on to brew, you fiddled with the buttons on my flannel. Lane said, "I don't have any cream."

"Black is fine."

She rolled out an *Oh* sound, said, "Well look at you, all grown up."
"I've been trying."

Cracking her knuckles, she said, "Better hurry." I held my breath in the second before she let slip a smile, saying, "Calm down."

We sat at her breakfast bar, the steam from our mugs drifting to the ceiling. I told her about Scranton, about the cold, tree-thick valley my grandfather's rambler was harbored in. I used to do my homework while sitting in the sunroom off the back of the house, looking through the screened windows up the side of a petite mountain. I bounced you on my knee as you picked apart a store-bought California roll, a speck of seaweed laminated in the spit on your lip.

You'd always been an adventurous eater, trying, with fervor, every dish I put in front of you, and later, in those afternoons we spent together while your mother worked, we made a game of trying new foods. We'd walk up the tapered streets of HDF and stop into restaurants to split something. Your favorite was the Devils on Horseback from Izzy's, used to pop the date free from the bacon and eat them individually, made your hands a mess. This was when you were five, and I picked you up from kindergarten. Lane had been promoted to the head of her department, and since my classes were all finished by noon, I'd watch you. You were never afraid to eat anything I ordered. Yet, you wouldn't walk near any street without holding a hand.

Lane and I got by for years chasing the idea that what we'd created in her rowhome could be maintained simply by believing in it. At first, she'd call me after she put you to bed, and we'd sit in her living room drinking pinot noir. No matter how awake we might be, she sounded exhausted when she asked me to come to bed. I could tell she was more interested in the attention than me, but I didn't mind providing it. If I knew, was it still unhealthy?

The night I moved in, after I got my clothes situated in the basement, Lane had reclined on the couch with an Auden collection propped on her stomach. She'd wanted me to read it to her—it was her favorite book. But I knew your father bought it for her, and so I couldn't take part. I busied myself gathering your toys in their designated play-bins, moving about the room like I wanted to leave and staying so that we wouldn't fight before bed. Mine was a small rebellion. She read aloud to me, stanzas about the soul, the body, positions in relation to each other, her voice rising as she read the line—*In their ordinary swoon.*

I hadn't been listening. Or I had, but I didn't get it, so I said, "That's pretty."

"Which part?"

I'd just turned twenty—in arguments, she challenged my maturity as a means to back me down from a fight, and the years that followed, it was successful. I said, "The language. The language is pretty."

She nodded and turned the page to another poem, reading under her breath. Then another. Then she flipped back and muttered a line, over and over. *In their ordinary swoon.*

Tomorrow, it would rain. I'd felt the heavy atmosphere with my hand stretched out my car window, drifting home through traffic. I gathered your vinyl rain boots, your clear umbrella, placed them by the door. Lane said, "What do you think that means?"

I didn't know, and I couldn't bring myself to tell her that I didn't know. As I sat at her feet, she closed the book. Looking back, that sort of give-and-get was how we functioned. Or maybe that's what I told myself about it—what we had wasn't necessarily special, or passionate, but it was comfortable, and that comfort had worth. When it was over, some years after that night, she said, "He's been clean for three years. I have to give him another chance." I'd be lying if I said I didn't cry, that I told her that I loved her in that way people do that sounds like they are begging for their life. Lane said real love is wanting the best for someone, even when that precludes yourself. I didn't want change, to be expendable. Through

the night, our argument grounded itself in Lane's words, like a
mantra—"He's Carl's father."

~

I don't think of my dad. By the time he came back around, I was
sixteen and had grown enough without him. We'd get dinner
every few months—the distant way we spoke to each other, it was
like we were old friends held together strictly by the duty of having known each other once. He'd been in therapy for his anger but
had developed arthritis in the discs in his back. The VA gave him
morphine to cope. Every conversation was a string of things that
he was going to do, but nothing followed, leashed by the strength
of his high, and he cherished that high, seduced by the compla-
cency it allowed him—the VA disability pay, the days hidden away
in his apartment with his cat. When I think about calling him, I
get distracted by the idea that he is *my* father—if he wants to be
close, it's his role to chase me, to care for me.

    We are strangers to each other, and in this same way, you won't
know me. There is kindness in that, small and unnecessary. You
won't know that after I left, I spent five years ignoring myself,
working two jobs to pay for grad school, moving back home with
my mother.

    Then, I met June at a conference in Boston. We'd exchanged
hundreds of work emails over the years. As she shook my hand,
she looked at me as though I'd returned from the dead—her pale
lips pulling into a smirk, a touch of rouge blooming on her cheekbones. We were low-tier analysts at different branches of the same
company. After a dinner with our colleagues, we got lost looking
for the subway. A storm had blanketed the city in a thick, wet
snow. As the two of us trekked ankle-deep in the slush, I pulled
the pack of cheap cigarettes from my too-thin coat, handed her
one, apologizing for the quality. She said, "Oh, it's fine—I only
smoke when I'm away from home." We wandered off the busier

stretches back into a neighborhood where the cars hadn't been dug out. The porch lights fixed along the rowhomes' front doors turned the snow to amber and her cropped hair from brown to gold. We'd been trading pained stories as a way of getting to know each other. I said, "The house I grew up in had lanterns just like that on the stoop. My mom used to turn them on when it was safe to come home."

"And what if she didn't?"

My shivering hid a shrug. We waited at a crosswalk, followed a cab toward a busier street, laughed as the tires from passing cars flung water at us. I said, "I should've walked you back this morning."

Her lips smiled around the filter. "I made it just fine."

I rubbed my ungloved hands together, missing the warmth of the bar—our mutual acquaintances huddled in a booth near the kitchen, the two of us seated by the pool table. I'd been rolling the base of a pint glass in circles on the oak. June took my wrist and held it, knuckles to the wood. She drew letters on my palm like she was sending me a hidden message, but the words were upside down. "My dad told me that my mother was a palm reader," she said. Under the table, she closed her knees around mine. A boxing match was playing on the TV over my shoulder. I could see the jabs of the red gloves reflected in her eyes. She said, "I never met her."

When we finally made it to the stop, we missed the first train, had to wait for the next. We sat in the joint of it where the cab bent with each turn of the rail carrying us toward my room. On the plastic bench, June tipped her head to my shoulder as if we'd been here before, and she knew this was the part of our trip she could put her weight on me. Straightening my posture, I cherished that moment of support. It wasn't the last train, but it felt like it—the handful of passengers flirting with sleep, streetlights dragging lines across the black windows. The shins of my jeans were damp, her boots spotted with melting snow. I said, "When my dad was gone, we were broke. No food. Church clothes in trash bags. Dollar store Christmas. I remember asking my mom for seconds, how her voice pinched when she said *No, baby.*"

"Your poor mother," June said, "That would've killed me."

"I hated her for it."

Her right hand was engulfed between my palms as I tried to rub warmth into it. She told me I'd been too young to know better, but remembering it sat heavy in me. Work had put the analysts from my branch up in a hotel in the Financial District, the kind of place where the doorman removed his flat cap as he pulled back the handle of the entry, saying, "Welcome home." In the elevator, she kissed me on my Adam's apple.

"My father left me in a hotel bar once," she said. "He'd hit it off with the waitress and figured I'd be okay watching the Ray's game while he went up to the room."

"Beer and a ballgame isn't so bad."

"I was eight." She raised a fist to me playfully, and I flinched.

The night before had been earnest—two strangers waiting for something to go wrong. When it didn't, the very success of it had been exhilarating. She'd said, "Where've you been hiding?" I held her, wrapped in the sheet, feeling, in that moment, unafraid. Tonight, she dropped her coat on my suitcase, sat at the foot of my bed, and let me remove her boots. Sitting on the white comforter, the way her freckles decorated her pale skin, it felt like I was witnessing my own personal sky. I skinned her jeans from her legs, bit her on the curve of flesh above her knee. She said, "It's been so long since someone was hungry for me." Her cesarean scar was hidden in the folds of skin indented by her waistband. I kissed that ruddy line, the swell of her hips, wanting to leave an impression pleasing enough that maybe, one day, she might allow me to retrace it.

When we were done, I opened my eyes to the now-dark room. She became an arrangement of small points gathering the ambient light—a white tooth, a steel nose ring, her blue eyes wet, reminded me of the color of raven's wings in the predawn sky, how they gathered around the dumpster behind the grocer as I dug through discarded produce, looking for something edible to bring to school. My ear to her collarbone, I could hear her heartbeat slowing. I said, "What's it like to be with you? I mean to really *be* with you."

"It's a lot of obligations," she said. "I'm no fun."

I said *fun* was overrated, that being boring is better with company, and June grinned a birth—cheeks creasing to make way for her lips, her teeth. She said, "It would be."

I woke when she asked me how much later my flight was, the sun still low in the curtains. She was already dressed, and I felt self-conscious as the fabric of her attire rubbed against my naked body. I'm not someone who attracts people. I'm not magnetic. I've had to chase every relationship in my life. Yet, I tire so quickly. It's always been easy to look back and see the worth in the moments I no longer have access to, but to feel the value of something while contained by it—I was blind. I thought of you when I lied to June, when I said my flight was soon, that we should split a cab. Standing in the airport, she slipped my boarding pass from my pocket, saw that I wouldn't depart for another six hours. I said, "What's the harm?"

Later, before she boarded, June said, "It's not crazy to think it could work, is it?"

"Would you wait?"

"Where am I going to go?" She hefted the strap of her duffle bag over her shoulder. Her eyes edged with red, and in them, I saw a fear that resonated in me. She stepped toward the line, and said it again, trying to lift her tone with a lilt that sat strangely in her throat. "Where am I going to go?"

∼

It's hard to think that the last time I saw you, you didn't know I was leaving. We were at Izzy's, had just eaten duck hearts pan-seared in butter and thyme, served on toothpicks. Our homework was spread on the checkered tablecloth, and after I helped you with your spelling, you started drawing birds in a field. When Izzy wasn't cooking, he'd come out and chat with us. He'd grown fond of your appetite and my willingness to bring you there. That day, you asked him if we could buy hearts from the market so we could make the dish ourselves, and he said of course not—they don't sell duck hearts at the grocery store. He put his hand on my shoulder blade, grinning, said, "Besides, I can't afford to lose my best customers."

Your voice pitched as if you didn't believe him. You said, "Sure we can, they have all kinds of meat at Giant."

Izzy said, "Just the hearts? You go ahead and try, mister."

You lined up your colored pencils in front of you, said, "Where do you get them?"

I said, "He buys whole ducks, Carl."

You picked up a pencil, started drawing the sun over your landscape. "They're so small. You buy a whole duck just to get that little bit?"

Izzy had a laugh like a car starting. He said, "What do you think goes into those ravioli your mom likes so much? What do you think was in that terrine you ate last week?"

"I don't know," you shrugged. "Chicken?"

We laughed, and Izzy mussed your hair. You put your brown curls back in order. As he headed back to the kitchen, he cleaned his fingers on the towel tucked in his apron strap. We came out of Izzy's, and you stuck your hand out, instinctively, waiting for me to take it before you stepped off the stoop. Your hand was cold and damp, felt like a ball of metal against my palm. We got in my old Toyota that your mother couldn't believe was still running. I'd dropped a grand into the transmission, but everything else worked fine, and you liked it because the rear window went high enough that you could see the sky from your car seat. I kept a bottle of hand sanitizer in my cup holder, would clean my hands before I drove. If I'm being honest, the thin film of food and spit that constantly lined your hands bothered me, and I used to dread the moment you reached out. That morning, while you were at school, I loaded my clothing into the trunk. I didn't know I could fit the mass of my possessions in the trunk of a two-door.

I helped you get your backpack straps over your shoulders and walked you across the street. On your stoop, you yanked your hand free from mine, and I said that I was going to run some errands, that I'd see you later. I'd never lied to you before, but I needed the mercy of that escape. You didn't notice—your mind on home, your video games, the chili that Lane was making. I could smell the cayenne pepper from the front step, and when you opened the door and passed over the threshold, a whisper of her crept out, maybe in the dining room setting the table, or in the bathroom washing her hands. At once, the choreography of movements through your home was familiar and fleeting—slowly, a step will change, and then another, and the only thing I'll know of it is a memory, and can you hold a memory? Can you raise it up?

~

It took seven months and a pay cut, but I got transferred to June's division in Tampa. In that time, we emailed through the day, spoke on the phone when she could find time after she put her son to bed. Twice, I flew to Florida to spend a day with her while her ex-husband had visitation. She was waist-deep in her divorce, had so little time between adjusting to full custody and getting her son into pre-K that, the months before my move, we spoke less and less. My last visit, she'd said I shouldn't resettle for her alone, but I told her that I needed a change in setting, that I felt stuck in DC, that the vestiges of older lives were too heavy. We'd gone to the Dalí museum in St. Pete, spent the afternoon walking along the water, drank Modelos at a corner bar. I'd told her about you before, that my ex had a son whom I spent years with. Sitting on the patio, looking across the beach to the thin strip of opaque blue water that underlined a blood-red sky, she said, "It wasn't a relief to you?"

"Sure. Not, at first, but a while later," I said, peeling the gold foil off the neck of the bottle. "It never felt like work. Or maybe it did. It's easy to forget inconveniences. How they felt."

"That's definitely a luxury," June said. "We're going to have to pull over on the way back. Clear beer makes me piss a lot."

When we got in the rental car, she put her hand on top of mine. I said, "I think I've just always been so willing," and she leaned across the console and rested her temple on my shoulder. For forty minutes, we drove in a silence that became the purpose I'd been missing since those afternoons with you. A few months later, my first day in her office, she met me in the stairs on the way to our floor. It had been ten days since we spoke, but I was propelled by the memory of that quiet. June started a dozen different conversations, leaning off her perch on the step above me. When I put my hand on her waist to steady her, I felt her flinch at my touch—a slight, electric pulse from her hipbone, through her belt loop, into my palm.

"I should have told you sooner," she said. The air in the stairwell was strange and warm. "I'm sorry—I didn't think it was going to last. But he lives down the street."

After work, I drove to my two-bedroom and parked in the space designated for my address. Evening descended with the pulse of car horns from the neighboring highway and the grating sound of planes cutting toward TPA somewhere distant on the naked horizon. I'd wanted to be angry, but I understood June was protecting herself, her family, knew it in the same way that I know I'll disappear into my too-big condo and wait for a small change to unbuild me. Sitting in the car, it's hard to know I won't be anything for you. I'll just be someone who held your hand once while you were afraid. *Cuidado. Take care.* The streetlamps in the corners of the lot bring light to the night encroaching on my car. And though I know that no one is waiting, I can't bring myself to linger.

〜

Donut Man

When he woke me, it was still dark. I'd been curled into the passenger seat of the van while he stripped and waxed the tile of a Jiffy Lube. 'Beak,' he said. 'Let's get after it.'

'It' was money. I knew because, for the past few months, we'd spent our unsupervised visitations working one of his businesses. My father never had a steady paycheck. His odd jobs rewarded only hustle. I was nine—when I stayed with him, he'd sleep through the afternoon while I read for school or played Gameboy, then rush me through dinner to make it to a flooring job. We showed up late after the businesses had closed. I'd help him unload the van, sometimes sweep or mop, but I was too young for the thin hours of the night. When I got tired, I lay down in front seat, the whir of cars lulling me to sleep as they passed. There were days I'd wake up while we were on the go, unaware of the movement, but on nights when the job ran long, nights like this one, we went straight to the donut factory.

This was before Krispy Kreme had their own stores, before they had a station in every Giant and Safeway up the coast and still garnered interest in their rarity. Guys like my father—hands raw from disinfectant, the soles of his New Balance slick with wax—showed up with the sun to stuff their vehicles with the green and white boxes, hoping to resell them and pocket the markup. It was the Saturday before Thanksgiving, and holidays made for easy sales, but even so, I knew we'd have trouble unloading the amount he insisted on buying.

His Aerostar van was a windowless smoky black with the chrome stripped off. While he loaded boxes in the back of it from floor mat to bare ceiling, careful to keep everything separate from the mop buckets, the floor buffer, I watched the workers make donuts in the back of the factory through the viewing window. The circles of dough drifted along in a river of oil, starting soft white, dropped straight from the dispenser and ending on the drying rack, golden-brown, the sugar coming up in fumes.

'Beak, get your face off the glass,' he said. He called me 'Beak' because, while we were both Chinese, I hadn't yet grown into my mom's British nose. My father and I hadn't spent more than a weekend together since the divorce four years prior. He took his billfold from his pocket, peeled off a couple ones and handed it the floor manager who knocked on the glass and held up two fingers.

On the other side of the window, the bakers wore plastic aprons and latex gloves, hairnets and safety goggles. They took two donuts straight off the conveyer belt, slid them in a wax paper sleeve and brought them out to us. The heat of the pastry in my hands created a hunger I hadn't known, and I swallowed the donut in three bites. It was barely solid, so sweet it made my teeth ache, and I wanted another immediately.

'When was the last time your mom fed you something this good for breakfast?'

I was too busy licking the glaze off the back of my teeth to think about my usual breakfast—the off-brand cheerios dense as cardboard wet with rice milk, both donated from the church my mother dragged me to. Depending how far we were from her last paycheck, the meals became less complex. At first, pasta, home-made sauce, sautéed vegetables, salted chicken, and a week later, plain rice, canned tuna, soy sauce for flavor. Those meals, she'd stir her food between bites, as if it were hiding beneath it something worth savoring. I often tried to choose relative hunger instead of clearing my plate. We'd push it back and forth between us on the table until she'd slam a fist down, saying, 'Eat dammit. I don't work this hard for you to spit in my face.' There was something raw in her plea. When the dishes stopped rattling, her voice cooled. 'I'm sorry, baby. Please.'

Our route took us from the factory back toward his basement studio. We used to hit the strips of business parks and car lots congesting the main roads reaching out from 495 and the District. Rockville, Gaithersburg, College Park, Laurel—any hospitality service that needed giveaways or a staff that might want breakfast. The spots my father sold to often, the receptionists would declare 'Donut Man!' as we came through the door, boxes stacked on my forearms. When we entered somewhere new, he said it himself. At a car dealership, he leaned against the counter, speaking to a woman on the other side. The Tag Heuer watch hanging from his wrist was older than me. One time my mother joked that it'd been in and out of pawnshops as often as my father had been in and out of jail. The mention of prison took the humor from her face.

'Mind your manners, Jason,' he said. 'Tell Miss Cindy hello.'

As a kid, I'd been mild in temperament—bad at making eye contact, prone to long passages of silence—but we were a father/son sales team, and part of that act required me to smile when addressed. I'm not sure when my big-gummed grin became genuine, warmed by the attention. I said hi as my father opened the box on the top of the stack. Miss Cindy looked at the variety dozen, then me, saying, 'Well I don't know which is sweeter.'

We set the donuts on the counter, folded bills, returned to the van to restock.

My father only really taught me two things in life. The first was how to take money off people who had it to spend. We were on the beltway, and he decided we could sell more if we split up. Awake all night cleaning floors, he was beginning to fade as the day wore on. He wouldn't admit it, but his eyes were ringed red, and we'd barely made a dent in the product. I was worried that no one would want to buy from just me—no jewelry, no swagger or familiarity—but he assured me, saying, 'All you got to do is treat them like you love them. Bat your eyes a little. If they don't want to buy, hey, no sweat, see you next time. Thanks anyway. You can't *make* anyone do anything.'

The next stop in Tacoma Park, he gave me enough cash to make change, then put me out on my own. We priced a dozen glazed at ten, the assorted boxes of jelly and chocolate and Bavarian creams for thirteen, one of each for twenty. I kept repeating this pitch in my head as I went into the stores. My first few attempts—a laundry mat, a RadioShack, the Post Office—were met with polite rejections. I was too courteous, entering silently and waiting in line. The mail clerk behind the glass barricade looked at the boxes, then over my head and toward the door before saying no with a smile. I crossed the street, my arms shaking a bit under the weight of the boxes. There was a bank on the corner, and as I approached the wide, double doors, a woman held one open for me, saying, 'Aren't you precious.'

Part of me worried I was moving too slowly, that I'd have kept my father waiting and his impatience would turn to anger or disappointment. Part of me worried I'd come back without making a sale. I walked past the velvet ropes and the stanchions that formed a queue to the tellers toward a man sitting at the desk in the middle of the lobby. I said 'Krispy Kreme!' when I was within ear shot. He said, 'Well what've you got here?' and I gave him the pitch, the pricing. The bank manager was older, his hair thin at the temples, silver roses patterned across his tie. He told me they had a meeting coming up in an hour, and wouldn't it be nice to provide some refreshments for the brokers and reps that morning? He bought everything I was carrying, and I skipped back to the van waving the cash like a trophy.

My father had just closed the sliding door. When he saw me, he snatched the money from my hand, a bit of spit coming off his lip as he asked me if I was stupid. He said, 'You know the best way to lose something, Beak? Let someone know you have it to lose.'

In the passenger seat, I shrank into the cushion, resting my head against the doorframe. He closed the door and sat, joining the money I'd earned with the roll in his pocket. Before he dropped the van in gear, he took his bifocals off and polished the dust from the lenses. He said, 'You need to know how to be careful.' Always count the money by the door. The trick is to keep small bills on the outside and stow it in your front pocket where it's hard to get to. The skin on his knuckles looked like worn leather sliding into his jeans, his old graduation ring studding his pinky. To this day, I've never misplaced a bill.

Each stop, we split up. Halfway around the beltway, I came back from my rounds to find him napping. With the holiday around the corner and a bit of encouragement, people were looking for excuses to indulge. The ease of the sales only fueled this new confidence. Each time I sold out and came back to the van—that money rolled in my pocket—I was fired up.

Eventually, my mom would lock him up again for falling too far behind on the child support, but just then, I rode shotgun, a stomach made for sugar and a newfound love of counting cash. Stop after stop, while he napped, I hefted the donuts into my arms, brought the boxes into doctor's offices and furniture stores, real estate headquarters and used car lots, pulling back the glass and saying, 'Krispy Kreme!'

I woke him when we needed to move, and halfway around the beltway, I sold the last dozen glazed to a dentist off Route 1. The wad in my pocket was so thick my pants fit tighter. I knuckled him in the bicep, and he rubbed his eyes, pushed his bifocals up the bridge of his nose. He said, 'Where to?'

'Home.'

'We've got work to do, Beak,' he said. The cough in his waking throat sounded thick with mucus. 'Where to?'

'Home,' I said. 'They're all gone.'

Maybe it was exhaustion, but the wrinkled brow, the pinched confusion of his expression made me feel like I was lying to him. He turned in the seat to the belly of the van, empty now except for the cleaning supplies, the comforter that covered them. When he smiled, I could see the gold crowns glowing like embers in the back of his mouth. He dropped the van into gear and put us on the road.

On good days, we'd get wings and rib tips from a Chinese carry-out around the corner from his place. We'd each eat half of one dish then trade. Side by side, in the front of the van, we ate until our forks scraped the bottom of the styrofoam trays, until we unbuttoned our jeans to get comfortable.

'Your mother and I used to live above a spot like this in Wheaton. The kitchen was below our bedroom. Just the smell of chicken would turn her stomach, but you know, I was always craving it,' he said. 'I bet she still doesn't let you eat it.'

'She says eating out is a waste of money.'

Cartilage from the pork cracked between his teeth, and he grunted the bone into a napkin.

My arms, my feet, ached from the hustle. In the driveway, we instinctively opened the sliding door on the van to carry in what we couldn't get rid of—the donuts we would eat for dinner. But I'd sold us out. In my pocket was the proof. I showed it too him—the roll of bills suspended between us bulging out my fist, and I felt alive.

'Hey, Donut man,' he said standing over me, inspecting the features of my face. I could see my reflection in his glasses, distorted by the curve of the lens. We were so much the same except for those small and important differences that are lost when the eye isn't focused—how I don't fully recognize myself now when it's four in the morning and I'm washing my face in the sink after a shift, the tips in my jeans still damp from the beer-slick bar; how, tired and worn thinner by liquor, I look out the window and can't tell if the sun is coming soon or just gone. With his finger, he tapped me on the nose, saying, 'Hand it over.'

⮎

Once You've Gone Back Home

They'd gathered to watch Hao sing—his first public performance. There'd been fractions of rehearsals, drunk nights in a dim living room, a few songs to end the night after the beer ran out, but never a stage. I only went to get more time with Tulsa and sat next to her at the back counter, looking at Hao through the beer taps. A Stratocaster belted to his skinny-jeaned hips. His neck craned to the low microphone. Fresnel lights thumbed a shadow across his long face. Six-string chord changes droning under his Johnny Cash drawl, he sang slow enough to rake you with confessional lyrics, always a clever turn in the refrain, and that was the difference between us, I didn't know how to be clever. We'd come up in a garage band together, playing little basement shows and bar gigs for free drinks. That trailed off sometime before he and Tulsa started dating. Then it was all smiles and *Hey sweetheart*, never one without the other. Their comfort—boothed across from it in restaurants, elbow-to-elbow with it in bars, how they communicated in glances as if words were an afterthought—had been an eighteen-month sprained ankle for me, a nagging reminder that I was unfamiliar with that ease.

Or maybe I was just jealous of him. We'd been something like inseparable once—those friends who often bickered until stumbling on an old joke and silently forgiving each other. He used to call me a brute cause I'm the stocky sort of Chinese. My mother said our people belonged on the water—thick-necked and short-limbed, dark skin begging for sun—that it takes a specific strength to drag the nets against the tide. Told me this when I got expelled from the ninth grade in Cambridge for fighting. I was heading to Fenwick to live in my aunt's trailer on the coast, just south of the state line. I'd been there ever since. My aunt passed a couple years back. I remember thinking, *That's something,* while I gripped the new deed to her place, my name adrift in the lines of bold print.

Hao lived two docks over, separated by the bay's green fingers. When we met, I was convinced we'd always be the odd men out and daydreamed about heading west to DC, or up to New York where being Asian wasn't something of note. He was hesitant to believe it, said I was just imagining myself as an outsider. There was German in his blood—he was taller, fairer, made friends easily. As teens, we'd leave his stuffy trailer after band practice and lie on the docks, smoking my aunt's Virginia Slims. Sometimes, she'd sit with us while we talked about the songs we'd never write. She didn't care if we drank her liquor, and two pints of MD 20/20 in, Hao said when he was a kid, he used to think the chirps of the crickets were the stars whistling, trying to get his attention. He raised his arm toward the sky, pretending to pinch one faint glow between his thumb and forefinger. I yanked the bottle from his other hand, said, Someone's had enough. The chalky liquid churned in the bottle, and my aunt smiled, told me not to be jealous and left her cigarettes on the foldout chair.

Now, in the bar, Hao began a song about his first love—a girl from Philadelphia. She'd just graduated, had come to the beach for vacation. Her inevitable return home made them move quick, and at that pace, they found something like meaning. Hao said, She left for home and my home was here, in the scene of that momentary obsession. Tulsa asked me what she'd been like, and I said she was pretty—real pretty—the kind that lingers. The way Hao went about singing it, with contempt for his younger self, all of those summers before we turned twenty-one seemed foreign.

We'd been lifeguards since eighteen, used to walk home from the beach, passing a water bottle full of vodka between us, won-

dering whether we'd ever get tired of the tourist months. We figured we would but hoped against it. The sun rubbed light on the
hem where the sky sank into the bay, the distant thump of hip hop
in motel rooms lining the road. I threw my arm over Hao's shoulder while three girls and a dude came the opposite way. The guy
said, Hey where's the party? Their bathing suits were still water-
logged and dusted with sand. I raised the bottle toward his face,
and he smelled the rubbing alcohol scent of the Rikaloff, said, Oh
shit. Hao said, Help yourself. They followed us to a good strip of
beach north of the boardwalk, one where businesses didn't shine
their patio lights out toward the ocean. We sat in the dark on our
towels and played Sip-Sip-Pass until the vodka ran out.

There's nothing like the ocean at night—the break of the waves
unfettered by gull calls or the crowds conversing. Hao showed the
girls the stick-and-poke tattoo of a mallard he'd stitched onto his
bicep. They circled around him, asked him how he did it, and he
recreated the process with a barb of driftwood for a needle, a palm
of water as India ink. I stood, joints loose from the booze, in the
wet sand with the foam of the wake lapping at my feet. A chill
breeze rushed past, and I felt like I was standing on the lip of a
mouth, the slow exhales of something giant. I knew how quickly
the ocean could eat you. That fear of fragility—of being swallowed
up against my will—had burned like fuel in me, was what made
me say *Yes* in the face of self-doubt. I figured I spent too much
time in the Atlantic, that one day the water would catch me off-
guard, and I'd be damned if I didn't live a life before it got me.

We're twenty-six now, and I still get that fist-tightening excitement when summer begins. Route 1 steadily swelling with packs
of sandal-wearing families, a herd of college kids, new faces rushing toward the breaking waves. Every week a shuffling of the
cards, and Hao and me, we'd been there all along.

∼

Tulsa changed that rhythm. Nights when we'd go to the busier bars down near the single digits, she'd tag along, and then there was no more flirting with vacationers. I used to tell people I only lived there for the summer. At a club, I got a number, and Tulsa leaned against the counter, said, Who wouldn't want to call the beach home? She didn't understand. These people didn't need to know that when they left for the winter, I went back to chasing shifts at the bar, to off-season work scrubbing empty hotel pools, the cleaner eating my cuticles. Few years back, Hao started teaching guitar up in Rehoboth. He was making steady money, year-round work. And with Tulsa waiting for him after his lessons, he stopped grabbing the bus with me downtown.

It changed with our friends when he was absent. That first question as I sidled up to the circle—*Hey, where's Hao?*—annoyed the shit out of me. Still, I was relieved to be away from their coupling. I downed beer after beer with this image of them splitting Hao's beat-up leather couch, building a private life up like walls around each other. They didn't need me. And yet, they were not unkind, inviting me over a couple times a month to listen to records while Hao cooked. I'd bring a six-pack and drank my two as Tulsa asked me about us as boys. I said, We were the kids you wanted to know. You remember Sharkey's, man? Hao's sister used to date the bartender there, never carded us.

Hao was chopping onions, took a break to sip his beer, saying, Shit, whatever happened to Marcus? I haven't seen him since that place shut down. The belly of the trailer filled with the salt-thick scent of fat cooking off flank steak. I said, How many boardwalk girls you think gave us the time of day just cause we knew a spot to drink? Hao's face went flush, a chuckle low in his throat as he stared into the pan, stirring the vegetables into the meat. Tulsa reached over and mussed his hair. Well it certainly wasn't for your looks, she said. We talked into the night until the conversation became riddled with quiet gaps—a signal I'd come to understand as a marker for my exit, allowing them to return to that thing they could only occupy alone.

～

Just after Labor Day last year, Hao's car broke down, and he asked me to take him to work. I was done on the beach for the season, had the afternoons off, so we hopped in my aunt's pickup and headed north. He said, What're you doing for work now? You going back to Rusty's? Told him I'd gotten a job serving at a crab house, bayside. It did good business, even in the winter. He nodded, slowly, like he wasn't quite hearing me. The day was overcast, gray clouds blending into the pitch water visible through dips in the sand dunes. Hao's black hair was tipped with grease. I knew he'd been skipping the shower. When we were younger, we'd go a week without anything but ocean water and a quick rinse in the outdoor faucets stationed on the beach. The salt made our thick hair wavy and malleable, our skin dark and taut. We were creatures born of the sea. He looked out at the dunes, said, You think you can get me some shifts? I asked him if everything was alright, if he still had guitar students, and he said, Yeah, yeah. Of course. I'm just trying to stay busy.

No one could tell me why they'd ended it, but it had gotten around that they weren't dating. I'd be lying if I said that didn't well up some excitement in me. Worked out we fell back into our old habits without her—drinking till close at the bars we knew, talking about back in the day. I showed him some songs I'd been working on, and he did the same. It was clear how much better he'd gotten over the years with steady practice. I had to be bored to even pick up my SG. We spent more time with music, even talked about starting up a band again, and he said he'd think about it just as soon as he got his record done. He'd been trying to finish for years.

～

Tulsa talked to each and every person she met as if they were the most important being on her planet. It wasn't a surprise when our friends tacitly decided that she'd remain one of us—a group she could count on to gather at the beach near 130th, who'd invite her to family dinner every Monday and Industry night at Rusty's on Sunday. Tulsa hadn't come up in Ocean City like the rest of us, didn't know how to keep going in the cold months when the population dropped and the very blood of Coastal Highway slowed to a halt. You need to have people to help make it through the winter.

The audience huddled around Hao, as though for warmth. The half-full room was congested in front of the stage, set apart from the scuffed dance floor by a riser. The crowd clapped with each interval in the music, singing lyrics when they knew them. There was nothing flashy to his performance, nothing anyone hadn't heard before, and yet Hao had a way of twisting that familiarity to be heartfelt. I leaned over to Tulsa, said, It's really simple, isn't it? But there's something wounding to it. She hadn't looked at me since the set started. He's entirely honest up there, she said.

It happened, at first, unconsciously, that I wanted to elevate her in the way she raised others. That position was unfamiliar to me, and in its strangeness, I became absorbed in how the world I came up in *took* to her. The nights I wasn't serving, when I'd ask Hao to go to the bar and he'd turn me down to record, when I would end up going by myself, searching for easy company, I started inviting her along instead. Told myself I was just being a decent friend, a good person. Maybe that was true—if nothing else, it showed I hadn't just been her friend because she was dating Hao, that she was worth knowing. And yet, I am not a good person, have never really claimed that moniker. I'd always found that if I was honest with myself about what I wanted, those desires interfered with my friends' lives—couldn't work there because they fired this person, couldn't date her because so-and-so has a crush, can't play in that band because so-and-so got kicked out of it. It didn't matter if I acted on them. The urge itself condemned me. So it was unsurprising that I wanted to be in Tulsa's presence—her licorice black hair, those blue eyes, the way she burped halfway through a beer. I wanted to be the one she exhaled around.

We discovered a mutual love for pool, had a weekly game at the Sand Dollar where the drinks were cheap and the felt of the tables was red. Few years ago, she'd followed some skateboarder here from Baltimore. The plan was that he'd use the off-season months to practice, to shoot a promo video, then they could party through the summer. When he bailed, she got stuck with the lease, and by the time it ended, she'd found a paying job at a preschool and her coworker had set her up with Hao. We're shooting pool one night, and I was curious, so I nagged her about why she'd ended it, and she said, It was mutual. He's got such a decent heart in him, but that's not always enough.

I let her win a few games, bought the next round. Asked her again, saying, Come on, it's just me. Her expression looked more exhausted than trusting, but trust is a form of giving in. She said, Hao is good. He's talented and beautiful and good. We wanted it to work, but like, you can only spend so much time thinking everything would make sense eventually, you know? She paused to make the five in the corner, scratching the cue, saying, We weren't happy. I could sense her spirit folding as she said it, surrendering to those three words, and I didn't mean to take her there. I raised my drink off the end table after I missed a glancing shot, said, Well, now you're stuck with the rest of us lowlifes.

At pool, we'd kept a running record. The day of the show, I was up 58 to 41, but we hadn't played in a few months. When summer started, I got a call from my mother. My sister had been in a car wreck. I locked up the trailer, spent the hot months with my family in Minnesota while she recovered. In August, she swiveled in her bed and stood barefoot on the sterilized tile. My mother hadn't touched her while she was bedridden, even when the nurses said some contact was fine. She wore her wool sweater and slacks loose on her rail-like limbs, wringing her hands together instead of clearing sweat from her daughter's forehead or adjusting the part in her mocha hair, all for fear of worsening the damage. She'd always been like that, thinking she only made things worse. My sister, standing, reached for my mother, and they grasped each other's shoulders, knees shaking, fingernails digging. My older brother in the corner of the room, shouted, I told you! I told you! Over and over and I ached for him to stop, his words cutting ribbons out of this reunion. In the hallway, I said, You always do that shit. You always involve yourself in other people's moments.

I'd gotten that news in a voicemail while at work. Mom had caught the last flight out of BWI and booked me the only seat to Minneapolis the following day at three. I could've gotten a ride from almost anyone, but Tulsa and I were supposed to shoot pool that night, thought that was reason enough to ask her. It was two AM, and my call woke her. Told her about the accident, about the spinal contusion and the numbness in my little sister's limbs, how she couldn't support her own weight. She was a freshman at UM, the passenger in a car on the way home from a party. Driver didn't make it. I didn't even know you had a sister, Tulsa said. What can I do? I said, I need a ride to the airport tomorrow. My voice felt disconnected from my lungs as I spoke—worry for my sister made my heartbeat rap on my esophagus, yet part of me was still looking for an excuse to see her.

Tulsa showed up at my place too early, my flight was hours away. She knocked on the trailer window to wake me. I let her in and she examined what I'd thrown on my duffle bag—board shorts, a few T-shirts, the entirety of my clean underwear. She said, Have you ever been to Minneapolis? You need to pack some pants, maybe a sweatshirt. I did as I was told. She looked at me as if I were a stray limping out of the wilderness, hungry for compassion. She said to come on, that she was going to take me somewhere, then carried my luggage to her Civic. The bright red paint on her car used to annoy me. As we pulled out of the cul-de-sac, I couldn't bring myself to glance over but could still see, in my mind, the maroon trellises lashed to the side of Hao's trailer, the plastic awning yellowed by the rain.

Route 50 turned north before I asked her where we were going. She said, You just find an appetite. We spoke about my sister's health until every answer became *I don't know*, and then she talked idly about her job, about gossip, things she'd heard around the way. She said, So you're seeing Tina from Rusty's? She's pretty. I shook my head, said we'd gone out a couple times, but it wasn't right. The road toward the Bay Bridge felt like it was sinking beneath the rain-thick grass, as if the flat fields were soft enough to swallow up the cement. So you're more of a boob guy? she posted her left hand atop the wheel, right elbow on the middle console. I coughed out a laugh, said, It's not like that. Tulsa perched her chin atop her fist, head turned my way, eyes slipping from the road ahead. She said, I'd kill for her legs. I took it as an invitation to think of her lower half, a tattoo of an eagle shot full of arrows astride her right thigh, the scar from a bike accident on her left shin. I liked the way she crossed her legs at the ankle as she applied tanning oil, standing beside her beach towel, her back to the sun.

At the ascension of the bridge where the Jersey walls gave way to pale steel barricades, the road cleared the Chesapeake and climbed into the wet air. Tulsa rolled the windows down, the wind whipping her hair about her face. She let her left hand glide out the window—a flesh kite in the current—yelling over the roar of air racing into the car, This thing scares the piss out of me. She flinched, pulling her lips back, not in a smile, but a taut line, the uncomfortable expression of someone expecting pain. In the middle of the ten-minute bridge, under the framework where the barricades rise to a point out of view, it's easy to feel a caged sort of safety from the green water a hundred feet down. But on the incline, the decline, the barriers are just low enough to see the danger below. As a kid, shuttled across it, I felt no fear, convinced that no man-made structure allowed harm to those inside it. Looking over the side now, the girders throwing shadows across the red paint of the hood, I thought about when that semi struck a car last year, sent it plunging into the water. How that woman survived, I wasn't sure. I knew if it were me, I wouldn't be so lucky.

Tulsa pulled into a strip mall twenty minutes south of the airport, took the keys from the ignition, said, Hao ever bring you here? I shook my head, unfamiliar with the sandstone building, the cyan paint along the roof chipped and faded. The corner Chinese restaurant had a paper sign under the hours that read *Dim Sum Every Weekend.* My mother had taken the family to Dim Sum when I was younger, and I remembered, fondly, the draping smell of meat and oil, the pristine tablecloths, waiters pushing carts of metal steaming dishes that rattled as the wheel caught a lip in the carpet. I poured her tea and we pointed at the buds of shumai, shrimp dumplings, pork buns and taro pudding. The waiter stamped our ticket, piling the dishes onto our two-top. I shoveled rice into my mouth, said, I never realized how much I missed this. She had a cheek-full of garlic greens, a bit of sauce staining her lip. Another cart came and I shook my head at the tripe and the chicken feet, but Tulsa said we'd have both. She said, What? You're too good for scraps? She plucked two of the clawed feet from the bowl of broth, holding them above the table and walking them over to my plate as if the bird itself was above the cooked appendages. I looked at the orange limbs, greasy and lifeless, said they were gross. When she spoke, Tulsa looked almost embarrassed, saying, They're for your sister. It's a silly thought, I know. Feet for her feet. She glanced at the white table linen for a moment, and I nudged her shoe with mine, saying, Thank you. We ate every appendage to the marrow.

～

Two beers into the set, Hao played a slowed version of "Freak Scene" by Dinosaur Jr.—one of my favorite songs. We used to blast it in the trailer, headbanging on the couch until my aunt got off work. Didn't realize he liked this song that much, I said. I tapped my heel on the footrest, annoyed at how the lyrics still made my hair stand on end, that it was his mouth delivering them. When he got to the last verse, he lifted his head from the crowd, looked me directly in the eye. I couldn't tell if he was smiling, but I raised my glass off the bar toward him and he turned back to the micro-phone. Watching his forearm pulse above the guitar, pinched fin-gers strumming the gap above the pickup, I would be lying if I said I didn't want to be there next to him, playing the root chords, letting him embellish the melody, the solo.

When I got back to Ocean City, I called Tulsa to see if she was up for a night at the Sand Dollar, to catch up, and she asked if I was free that afternoon, said she needed to borrow the truck. I drove her up to Rehoboth to pick up a new mattress. Her last one was her ex's and she was tired of how soft it was in the middle, tired of wak-ing up with a sore back. We were walking through the aisles of the furniture store as she pressed her palm into the springs of each cushion. Plus, she said, There's a lot of old boy sweat in mine. I'm ready for a clean break. The thought of Hao's condensation in her sheets made me cringe, and the souring on my face made her laugh. I was not unaware that the two of us testing mattresses on Saturday afternoon resembled a couple. She said, I need some-thing that is firm enough to sleep on my stomach, but soft enough to spend the occasional day nesting in. I asked what that felt like, and she said she'd know it when she found it. She kept politely shooing sales attendants, eventually found herself stationed on a full-sized pillow-top in the window of the store. I was on my phone, texting people that I was back in town, and We should hangout sometime, watching her bounce on the foot of the bed, her lower back peeking out over her shorts. She collapsed onto it, looked at me from flat on her back, saying, Come here. I would be lying if I said that I didn't imagine, right then, what it would be like to fall asleep beside her, to feel her forehead, sweat-slicked, against mine, an hour of sex behind us—thinking *Fuck you, Hao*. Seated on the bare mattress, she said, What do you think? I pressed a hand into it, the springs below the top cushion barely gave. It's firm, I said. She grabbed a fistful of my shirt, fingers grazing my spine, pulled me alongside her. See? It's good right? The ceiling tiles above us were ringed with brown water stains. I could feel her breath churn.

I strapped it to the bed of my pickup, helped her carry it into her home. I'd never been in her room before, was surprised at how bare the walls were, her dresser drawers unclosed and bulging with clothing. By that time, I'd gotten a couple texts about the show, but I didn't mention it until she said, You know Hao is playing tonight, right? I nodded, seated on the bare mattress again, watching her riffle through shirts in the closet. I said, You going? She got to the last hanger, saying, I should really do laundry. Or clean up a bit. I shrugged, I think you look good. The springs had so little give as she sat down beside me. Rubbing her palms in her lap, she said, He stopped practicing while we were together. I feel like he wouldn't want me there. I slowed him down. When I wrapped my arm about her and touched her on her side, I wanted to will him from her mind, to reassure her, not that he wouldn't care, but that for as much as he might not want her around, I did. I said, I'll go if you go.

$\sim$

Hao's black hair was brimmed with sweat, the collar of his shirt flattened by the guitar strap. He looked wet and pink, as if he'd just come in from a run, and yet, basking in the attention of the audience, he belonged nowhere else. He said, This last song is a slow one. Not that any of my stuff is that upbeat. The crowd chuckled as he took the capo from the headstock and locked it to a fret, saying, It's called "Last Song for Sweetheart."

I couldn't tell you the words, just that the chorus lyric was the title phrase repeated twice, paced the first time and even slower the second. Hao's left hand dragging down three notes in a scale, his vocal following in harmony—I caught the look on Tulsa's face as he sang it, how she felt every word as if the notes themselves had hooks that flew from the amplifier, snagging her eyelids, her rouged cheek, the very curve of her lips. Twitches like microscopic explosions rippled through her expression, and I knew it as the face of surrender, of recognizing a love you once called home and all the ways it was given up.

Leaning into the bar, I could feel in my chest—was so sure— that I lacked those same barbs to harm her, that I could never eclipse the affection she'd already had, that love she wanted but not enough. I prepared myself for a crippling sort of failure at this, of loss or embarrassment, but found myself beholden to their faces as the song played on. To witness their mutual beauty, to know the circumference of what they meant to each other, and yet to be apart from it, still warmed me like hands over an exposed flame. Long after I moved away from the coast, after I gave up music all together, I find myself rehearsing that moment when they stepped briefly back into that world they built together—how it was there to come back to. It makes for a nice foundation to live upon—a center to raise my walls around, to house my unstill heart, and wait. The song ended, and she teemed with grief. The blue in her irises laminated with a near invisible sheen, and yet, Tulsa smiled. Without taking her eyes from him, she whispered, That's what's different. He wants everything painful to be pretty.

Gramps

When they shot your second wife, you fled Carolina and gave your life to horses. This was well after you changed your name from Roy to Gerald cause you didn't want to be a cowboy in law school. Now you're mucking your own stalls. You told me that story as I learned to heft a shovel, throwing manure into a wheelbarrow. I filled up the feed, hosed in the water, liked the clop of their teeth as they chewed through the hay. Your farm was hemmed with Appalachian ivy that ran along the posts—held together seven pastures and the ankle of a mountain. After that Thanksgiving, your third wife didn't want us around, but while the cobbler finished in the oven, you taught me how to rap my finger on the electric fence to test the pulse. Asked you why that Appaloosa had his own lot, and you said he was still wild. Got him for a steal because you thought you'd break it, and now you're too tired for taming. This is how I knew metaphor before I owned the word, how I know now you're just sitting on the couch, listening to plums fall from the trees in your yard. You are, you are, you are, and when you're not, I'll remember you black and white, flat-capped, Lucky Stripe on your lip, snapping, *Get up six! Get up six!* Fist wrapped around a trifecta ticket, knowing when a horse had more to give.

⤸

Mongolian Horse

Andy had the top bunk, and I was below, liquor-dazed, letting her sister teach me how to touch. Carmen propped her head on the bottom rung of the ladder framing the bed, said, "Faster." Her fingers were rough from bartending, could feel the callouses on her palm against my temple. It was near morning, and we'd figured Andy had fallen asleep, that she'd got bored with the conversation when she heard us kissing. Her fingers knotted in my hair, Carmen pressed my face to the sweet and sweat-tinged smell of her. The pressure on my jaw made my TMJ flare up, put pain in the joint below my ear. My feet were hot, tangled in the knit Afghan folded at the base of her mattress, but I didn't want to move, to rock the loose wooden frame, to wake Andy.

When I dredge into the memory of that night, I can see their room unlit except the window shades struck yellow by the streetlight outside their third story window. Carmen's hips lifted off the mattress, and I moved with urgency, my forehead on the curve below her stomach until she placed her hands on my cheeks, brought me to her the way she might pool water in her palms and raise it to drink. I dried my hands, my lips on her comforter, and we lay breathing into each other's mouths. I said, "Did you?"

"You couldn't tell?"

I figured that saying nothing was better than having the wrong answer. She took my wrist, placed it on her crotch. Before I could ask what I was supposed to be feeling for, she said, "Just wait."

~

Earlier, when Sonar signaled last call with two flashes of the rafter lights, we trekked down Saratoga to grab a cab up Calvert. No bigger than Charles or Maryland Ave, Andy liked to call it "Calvert Highway" since the lights were more forgiving than other northbound routes, letting you get uptown quick. Andy's the younger sister, always flinging herself into new artistic endeavors. She'd learned to draw, then paint, had started tagging in Station North, sneaking out at three in the morning to spray paint murals of things like Frieda Kahlo as the Virgin Mary. The summer before, she'd taught herself to tattoo with a few lessons from her cousin and a bushel of grapefruit skins embroidered with ink. I met her when she got hired at the coffee shop in Towson where I'd worked in the interim between my bachelors and my MEd—two years when I couldn't pick a direction but knew that, at twenty-two, I still needed to move. She'd come down from Hanover to live with Carmen now that they both were single. It was a cramped one bedroom in Charles Village, and Carmen needed help covering the rent. They were always doing that—making turns in their lives at the same time.

After the first cab blew by us, Carmen adjusted her bra under her tank top and raised her hand out, waiting for the next. Andy, bent at the waist, tugged at the straps of her heels, all night saying how they cut into her ankles. She looked up, said, "Yeah that was the problem—your tits weren't out."

"Could it hurt?" Carmen said. I'd been standing between the two of them, caught a wink from her before Andy declared that there was no bearing it, unbuckling the clasps on her heels and stepping out of them. The kick drum was still pulsing in the soles of my shoes—how I knew I was drunk to the gills. We edged out onto the curb, our clothing loose and damp from dancing. They had three years between them but were similarly petite and olive tan, both with green eyes that sat like jewels on their ruddy skin.

In the last bit of fall where clouds put a boot on the city, they could pass for the kind of twins that purposefully pointed their style in different directions to establish uniqueness. Andy had a uniform, said she'd die in a loose T-shirt and tight jeans. Carmen had talked her into the heels, saying she missed those nights at the clubs when they were still toting fake IDs, dancing in their mother's stilettos. I took a few steps into the street, looking south to the Harbor, could see clear past the monument, the dim road vacant.

"Elton John is playing M&T tonight. That's probably keeping all the cabs downtown," Andy said. "We could just walk."

Carmen let her shoulders sag. "That's like sixteen blocks."

I said, "Might as well keep moving."

We set a path in the right lane, Carmen leading while I stepped backwards, watching for cars. Andy had to tiptoe around pebbles and glass, falling behind. I told her I could carry her if she wanted, but she swatted the air, said, "Oh please."

We'd gotten something like close when our schedules paired off—Monday to Thursday, opening the shop, stumbling in at four-thirty to warm up the espresso machines, to set up the pastry case, our manager in the back counting the tills. Ours was a commuter heavy spot—from six to nine, there was a line to the door—and we wrangled the drink bar, one of us pulling shots, the other handling the milk, pulling drip coffees, topping off Americanos with hot water. There was something pleasing about our efficiency, our ability to move, to create in tandem.

My car was in the shop with a busted head gasket, so earlier that night when we closed, Andy said she'd drive us to Sonar. I told her I could DD if she wanted, but she didn't mind staying sober. I was relieved—couldn't dance without being loaded. I'd been sneaking rum into my iced tea from the pint in my coat pocket just so I wouldn't be completely cold when we got there. Rum was her favorite—thought we could sit in the parking lot and drink it down before we went into the club. I sat on her trunk in the back alley where the overnight truck delivered milk and pastries at the ramp next to the dumpster. Andy blasted M.I.A., the bass rattling her open windows. She'd just learned how to six-step and was practicing, blackening her hands on the asphalt, waiting for Carmen to get off so we could head out.

Lately, before the steady flow of customers began, she'd told me she couldn't imagine anything new, so she'd taken to painting imitations—famous pieces of art with only flecks of her own style—a changed color here, a redrawn detail there. It's why she'd been turning to dance, to music, looking for ways to reinvigorate her creativity. I was half-asleep while, at my shoulder, she spoke low, almost whispered these intimate failings. The wax-paper lamps suspended beside the espresso bar turned her gold. I told her I didn't have much of an imagination, and she asked about the inspiration from my tattoos—from elbow to shoulder, a collection of emblematic images that now grouped together. I said that each was a long story. She pointed at the wishbone on my forearm, wanted to know if it could really be that deep, and I said, "Would you want anything that can be summed up in a word?"

Carmen worked in a college bar a few blocks down, had traded her closing shift that night for a double on Saturday. She was tough, could drink until last call and make it to work on time, hiding her hangover with a little eye shadow and an exaggerated pout in her lips. As she rounded the dumpster, duffle bag strap splaying her breasts, she walked with a form of confidence unfamiliar to me, like she didn't fear a judgmental eye but welcomed it. She knew how to put that idea into a patron's head—*yeah I'm your bartender, but I could be into you.* And I don't want to make excuses for myself, but if not for Andy, I could be in the herd of men spit-mouthed and star-struck, fawning over her every word. When the two of us drank at Carmen's bar, we'd sit at the stools along the backroom, had a good view of the counter. We'd watch college kids peeking as she bent into the cooler, looking down her shirt.

When she caught them, she sprayed them with a stream of water from the soda gun. She said to us, "It's funny—the more you shame them, the bigger they tip."

In the alley, Carmen got her hips rocking as the music hit her, tossing her duffle onto the car beside me, dropping into a B-Boy pose, one arm across her chest, the other hand on her chin, as if she were appraising her sister's new step. They motioned for me to join. The rum had warmed my chest, could feel the beat in my shoulders, my waist, but I was naked without the cover of darkness and wall of bodies a club provided. Sitting on the trunk, watching them dance circles around each other, reminded me of a time when I was a boy, uncomfortable with my leftover baby fat, wearing a T-shirt on the lip of a pool. But I wasn't thinking *Oh, poor me* either. Mine was a blood that required momentum—never been good at getting myself moving, but when Carmen grabbed my wrist, I let her pull me off the trunk. I'd learned to dance from my older sister. She'd perfected the art of the radio mix-tape, and when she'd collected ten tracks, she played them on repeat, taught me to feel the beat through a barrage of Salt-N-Pepa, Boyz II Men, TLC, saying, "All you need is rhythm."

I told that story to Andy the first time we'd gone to Sonar. Laughter turned her face to smile-lines and barred teeth. Leaning in, she shouted over the music, "Do you always think about your sister when you're dancing with me?" I swayed my hips now, the clap-snare and sub-bass of "World Town" clipping the car speakers and beating against the brick wall, picturing Andy moving somewhere behind me, even as her sister twisted and turned, inspiring me to loosen.

And later, on that walk back, past Mt. Royal and Penn Station, the *Male/Female* statue looming with its intersected spine bridging around a shared heart that glowed purple in the night—I plodded backwards, watching Andy navigate her bare feet through the debris. Down Calvert, pricks of light turned onto the street, and I

alerted them to the cars coming our way. We moved to the parking lane, waiting to see if there was a cab. When they were still
fifty feet off and we could see the vehicles were unmarked, Carmen turned up the street, the toes of her pumps grinding into the
asphalt. Andy lifted her right foot to her free hand, brushed pebbles loose from her sole. I put my back to her, hunched, said,
"Come on, tiny. Hop on."

"I refuse to be that kind of burden."

I wanted to say that I welcomed it, her burden, but instead just,
"We'll go until I'm tired, and then we can switch." She stepped
around me, walking on the balls of her feet. I could see where the
asphalt had dirtied them, said, "Look, you could stay stubborn,
and maybe we'll make it—slowly—there. But maybe you'll step on
some broken glass, a syringe, cut your feet all up. And I'll have to
carry you, getting your foot blood all over my jeans. Then Monday, I'll have to handle the bar by myself while you stand just pulling drip coffee because of your bandaged-ass foot."

The traffic light overhead changed from caution-yellow to stop
sign-red, put shine in the oil pooled around the gutters. Ahead of
us, Carmen was half a block up. Her hips still managed to swivel
with each belabored step. Andy looked left and right, checking for
cars coming on the cross street. She said, "If we can agree that this
is not a heroic act, I will consider it."

At her shoulder, I said, "Not heroic. Entirely practical."

"I should never have let you tempt me with Bacardi. We
could've driven home five times by now."

"Didn't exactly force you to drink it."

She adjusted the waist of her jeans, stepped behind me, and I
lowered to meet her. I braced for her weight, was surprised at how
little it encumbered me, and holding her off the ground that
moment before we trekked forward, I was relieved to know that,
while I am not strong, I was strong enough. Behind us, a train
swept under Penn Station, layered a steady rhythm of thudding

metal and wood to the chorus of distant car alarms. The curves of her inner thigh hugged the gap between my ribs and the crest of my hipbones. Her elbows just past my shoulders, I could feel her breath on my ear.

She said, "You know, you're not very comfortable. Too bony."

"Excuse me, I forgot to wear my saddle."

Leaning forward, her armpits atop my shoulders, hands joining in front of my chest, the dampness on the back of my shirt joined with the belly of her T-shirt. The rubbing of the two created a warmth that was neither hers nor mine but filled that place where our bodies met. She said, "I've never ridden an Asian horse before. I didn't know they existed."

"What do you think the Mongols rode?"

"No, I know. But like—what breed was that? Can you name it?"

"A Mongolian horse."

"You're making that up."

"I mean, it's not as sexy sounding as Palomino or whatever." I bounced her weight higher on my back, held the ditches of her knees in my palms. "But that doesn't mean it wasn't the horse. Almost conquered the world. That's more important than a name."

In the distance, a siren whirled, growing louder for a moment then fading away. She said, "I bet Genghis Khan was a good lay."

I made like I might buck her, and she put her cheek to mine, started clicking her tongue on her teeth like hooves in a trot. The smell of the rum on her breath, the sharp sound of taste buds pulled from enamel, sent the hair on my neck upright, and I could see only those teeth, square-topped and shaved down from a childhood of grinding her jaw while asleep. A customer had commented on how slight they were and while he topped off his coffee with cream, she bit down on her lips. I could tell she was self-conscious about them, and I'd never seen her shy away from anyone. So I told her about my TMJ, about how my jaw clicked when I opened my mouth too wide.

I took her hand, fingers coated with espresso grounds, and placed them on that loose hinge, opening wide so she could feel the grind of the joint on the cartilage. I said, "I'd be nervous to get in a fight now. One clean punch could shatter it."

She said, "Oh, that's why?" and smiled.

Carmen, a block away, had gotten to the red light at North Ave and turned, saw Andy on my back laughing, and stopped so we could catch up. We had six blocks till their building, and I wasn't sure I could make that distance with Andy's weight slowing me, but I wasn't ready to surrender it either. Andy pulled on my collar as we got to the light, sat back, said, "I'm fucking starving."

Carmen checked the time on her phone. "Everything's closed."

I said, "Korean barbecue stays open till four."

Andy tightened her legs on my waist, swayed back from me. I could see in our shadow stretched by the streetlight, she'd reached her arms out to our sides, elongated in silhouette. She said, "I haven't been to Jong Kak in a minute," said it like *young cock* landing hard on the *caw*.

Carmen rapped her phone on her knuckles, said, "I've got to be up at nine."

Andy said we could just meet up at their place, loosening her legs and sliding down. For a moment, in my fading drunk, my fingers held the tendons in her knees, unwilling to release. Carmen let out a sigh, her shoulders slack, said she was sorry, that she could use a sobering meal in these thin hours but wanted her bed. Andy embraced her, gave her a kiss on the cheek. There was a ritual to the shape of their embrace—whether hurried or lengthened, as if in anticipation of a long departure—it managed to recreate itself. Andy's arms reaching over, Carmen's hands hooking under, palms flat, filling the recess between her sister's shoulder blades. Andy would plant a kiss, a peck that came from the neck, forehead forward, pushing Carmen back as it landed. Then Carmen squared her hips with mine, and I could see her hipbones like staples bridging the space between her tank top and jeans. Andy stepped aside and started to don her heels, saying she could bear it for long enough to be allowed in the restaurant. A few cars passed on North Ave, heading toward Howard, and backlit by their headlights, Carmen's tan turned to slate, then pitch. Pricks of sweat dotted her hairline. She said, "C'mon Phil. Where's my kiss goodnight?"

Andy laughed, and I couldn't tell what amused her—the tone to Carmen's request, or the request itself, that I could be persuaded to slip from her. But the possibility that there was something to slip from felt like hope, and I've never trusted it, never raised myself up with it just to be dissatisfied. Andy wrestled the first heel on, and before she started the second, she joined in the pause between Carmen and me. I remember Carmen looked like experience, the skin about her collarbones taut and freckled, the muscles in her thighs creasing her jeans, how she tilted her head just so, pointing her chin my way. With Andy watching, I wanted to be able to stand—to strut even—to show her that I was capable. Andy must have seen all this passing over my face. She said, "Phil, don't be an ass."

Carmen bounced her eyebrows, the slight gap between her front teeth made pink with her tongue, saying, "Be a good boy, Phil."

The repetition of my name in succession sent blood rushing into my head, an unsteadiness like inebriation fueled by their attention. I'd never been allowed to feel beautiful. Andy didn't scoff, just chuckled almost too low to hear. She went to sliding her other foot into its shoe, dragging the strap across her ankle rubbed red from a night dancing. When I stepped toward Carmen, I like to think I still hadn't decided that it meant more to me to snatch up this opportunity to put my lips to hers—that it might never arise again—than to preserve that shred of affection Andy might hold for me. I believed that I could somehow have both, that the instance of that goodnight kiss would not disallow me from something less fleeting. And on the walk to Jong Kok, two blocks up, one block over, Andy didn't say anything that challenged this hope I'd disguised for myself as logic—that the small peck landing flush on Carmen's lips and the ease of Andy's daily predawn conversation were not, somewhere intertwined. I'm not sure why I thought I could keep both separate. We approached the backlit green awning, the Korean script printed across it a mold-yellow edging toward rust. Andy said, "Even the ugliest lights look like home in the dark."

In her ill-fitting stilettos, she passed through the threshold and smiled as if simply being in the restaurant had satisfied her hunger. Our waitress sat us in the back room away from the front door, secluded from the carryout counter and bathroom. The Korean barbecues in Station North always served after hours, so we got beers whose names we couldn't pronounce, split a massive order of spiced beef and a tofu hotpot. She said the last time she'd been here, it was on a double-date with Carmen and their exes. This was over a year ago, though it felt like longer, looking past my shoulder toward the kitchen where the smell of seared meat and vinegar plumed.

I said, "Do you miss it? Being in a relationship."

She posted her elbows on the table, craned her chopsticks over the small bowls of kimchi, pickled turnips, and steamed broccoli that formed an ellipsis between us. She said, "Not really. I left for a reason." She lifted a thread of cabbage above her head, let it dangle over her open mouth. As she chewed she said, "Besides, I can have him when I want. We still fuck when I need it."

I knew better than to flinch at that disclosure. I'd never met him, couldn't picture Andy with someone else's hands on her, but still felt a stirring in my chest—a jealousy toward something I couldn't imagine. Her eyes fastened to me just then, daring me to find discomfort in her frankness, to say something to question or condemn her choice. I pulled from my beer, the sweet barley of the lager mixing with the heat from the kimchi on my tongue. Our waitress set the entrees in front of us and asked if we needed anything else, folding her hands together. I asked her for a round of soju. The steam from the hot pot swung a curtain between us. Andy bulged her cheek with shredded carrot and a ribbon of beef, was still chewing when the shots arrived in chilled glasses. Our waitresses said, "To your health," and raised her hands, palm up, instructing us to drink. The burn of the clear liquor caught the chili and garlic spice coating my mouth, igniting it as I swallowed. I exhaled, pushing air from low in my gut, sipped my beer to scatter the spice. Andy kept her lips closed after she drank, bowed her head while the soju cleared her throat, knocking her fist on the table when it did. The handle on the cast iron bowl rattled. Andy said, "So much for sobering up."

The windows in the restaurant were covered with matte black paper. It was past three, and I was surprised how lucid I felt. During the week, when we worked at four-thirty in the morning, I spent the rest of my day in a stupor—sleep deprived and over caffeinated. But half-full with tofu and red broth, the last fumes of rum still coursing, I was present. When our waitress passed back through the room, I held up two fingers, pointing to the soju glasses.

"It feels good," I said, snagging a piece of beef from her plate, "the morning racing toward you and just saying *fuck it.*"

"Fuck a bedtime."

"Fuck well-rested."

"For the weekend, at least."

When we were finished, Andy went to stirring the residue of brown sauce and red vinegar, dabs of oil and broccoli dandruff with her chopsticks as if she were mixing paints. I still remember how her hands moved, how delicately she could bend those scraps into an image. We settled up, and she said she wanted to show me a mural she tagged a few weeks ago, said it was on the way back. I asked her how her feet were, if she needed help, and she said she was too drunk for blisters. A few cars raced south as we walked up St. Paul, ducking into an alley near the barrier where Station North blurred into Charles Village. Lamps mounted above the building's emergency exits lit the alley a muddled orange. Preemptively, I thanked her for letting me crash on her couch, and this amused her. I asked her what was funny, and she said just, "You're welcome."

The mural stood six feet high on the edge of the brick wall facing Calvert—a rendition of the Statue of Liberty with its eyeless face replaced by the UTZ chip girl, complete with helmet hair and that half-moon grin. We stood, basking under the flame of the spray painted torch. I touched the brick along the waves of the robe.

She shrugged, "Sometimes, I don't know what the fuck I'm going for."

Noticing a spot of dirt on the mural's hand where the fingers bent around the tablet, Andy licked her thumb and cleaned the olive paint.

I said, "Why'd you leave the tablet blank?"

"I couldn't remember what it said."

We stood close enough to see the fissures and chipped edges of the brick. The whir of a helicopter pulsed somewhere we couldn't walk to. I said, "Well, what do *you* have to say? Isn't that the point?"

The streetlights were coated with haze. She said she didn't have anything tender like that floating around in her, said it was time to get back to Calvert Highway. The liquor rested at the top of my stomach, felt like it was tipping into my lungs. I told her that wasn't true, that there was plenty gentle about her, she just kept it jailed up. Like a heart wrapped in a fist. She bunched her T-shirt and used the cotton to clean the sweat from her face, and I thought about how her bare stomach might feel under my palm. We turned onto the cross street, caught sight of a soapy light between the swath of trees planted in front of her building. I thought the moon had finally cleared the clouds until the search helicopter came into view from behind a neighboring walk-up, its spotlight lingering a moment before darting out of view. Andy limped to the threshold, saying with a lilt, "Home, home, home. And never the worse for wear."

On the old wooden stairs, her heels sent staccato knocks clamoring along the walls of the shaft above us. Carmen had dozed off on the couch. When I think about their place, now, what I see is the half-dead fern on their windowsill, the bottles of wine between the microwave and fridge, how you had to step sideways to get around the dining room table and into the pantry. That night, I couldn't make out any of those details in the dark room. The door clapped shut behind us, waking Carmen but only enough for her to untwine her legs and stretch out sideways on the sofa. Andy dropped her keys on the counter that separated the corner kitchen from the rest of the apartment, gestured for me to follow her into the bedroom, said, "Let's go to bed."

Andy stepped into the bathroom and ran water over her toothbrush, disappeared into the portion of the tiled room not visible from the bed where I sat untying my oxfords. She said Carmen wouldn't mind if I slept on her bunk. I unbuttoned my shirt, folded it on top of my shoes, deciding whether it would be appropriate if I removed my jeans and slept in my boxer-briefs. When I heard her pissing through the open door, I figured I was being squeamish, then sat in my undershirt and purple trunks, waiting for my turn to relieve myself. As she climbed the ladder into her bed, wearing only her oversized T-shirt, she looked at my underwear, said, "Aren't you colorful."

I brushed my teeth with my finger. There was something so pleasant about her teasing, and when I sprawled out across the bottom bunk, I let myself entertain the possibility that she would grow bored on her way to sleep and come down to kiss me.

When I closed my eyes, the room felt diagonal. Half-dazed, standing on the edge of a deep and unrelenting sleep, I thought the dainty shadow coming around the bedframe was Andy or a dream of her, that I had drifted off and revealed that wish to myself again unconsciously. It wasn't until her toes, still cold from the kitchen tile, touched me on the side, until she said, "Scoot over," that I knew it was Carmen. I never slept on my back, but I rolled onto it to make space for her as she collapsed, stomach down, into bed. I can see how that half-turn had been a form of submission, that I should've risen and gone to sleep on the couch, but at the time of the conceit, I was just staring at the support beams that roofed us in, absorbing the warmth of her upper arm. Time contracted, measured in the inches our bodies touched—at first, her shoulder on mine, and then, gradually, a forearm across my waist, her temple to my cheek. She exhaled before she kissed me, and with the fumes of her breath in mine, I became filled with exhaustion, like every hour of work, ever minute on the dance floor, each foot of that walk home caught up to me at once. Carmen tucked her hand into my waistband, pulled me back from sleep with a firm kiss, her tongue running across my lower lip. When she peeled back, the smack of suction and spit separated with purchase. Andy said, "Gross."

Carmen kicked the boards above us, said, "Go to bed."

"My ears are hissing."

"It was pretty loud tonight," I said. Carmen shifted onto her shoulder blades, hands folded on her stomach, knees slightly bent. The next twenty minutes, those hands shadowing my movements, landing on my body where I touched hers. The three of us talked about Sonar, how the crowd had thinned lately, about which songs they did and didn't play. Andy sang *We are, we're your friends. You'll never be alone again*, while I hummed the rolling bass line and Carmen thudded a kick drum with her fist against the bedframe. With Andy out of view, it was like talking on the phone, left Carmen and me free to do, physically, whatever we wanted, the act of keeping it quiet only adding to the thrill.

And I'd not known thrill then—inexperienced at twenty-two, having just come out of a long relationship with a woman who felt sex before marriage was a luxury. My understanding of it was encapsulated in half a dozen awkward and jerky evenings where the passion ran out before we were finished. Then I lay beside her, naked under the sheet while she questioned whether the failure of it had been a symptom of what she saw as a mistake. It reverberated in me as I kissed Carmen, eager to erase those letdowns, to prove that I was a man capable of familiarity, of pleasing. The conversation trickled, Andy's voice thick with sleep, and I put my mouth to Carmen's sternum, could still see the freckles scattered across her chest in the fog of the room.

She must have translated timidity from my movements—fumbling with her jeans, tugging at the straps of her shirt. Her back arched as she crossed her arms between us and freed herself from her tank top. Afraid to speak, she lead me with her hands, gently, framing my face, guided me all the way from a kiss to that moment some misplaced minutes later, my jaw aching while she held me by the wrist to the pulse between her legs. Carmen yawned, turned into me, saying barely, "See? You did that."

Sleep came for Carmen as soon as her arm was across my chest, right leg laced over mine, her weight pinning my back to the bed. Her breath in my ear, I focused on the how the street lamp outside backlit the blinds on their window. I stared, waiting for fatigue to overtake me. The plastic was swollen orange like the belly of a wood fire. The longer I focused on its glow, the deeper the surrounding room darkened. It was how I could see the whites of Andy's eyes grabbing color against the black backdrop as she lowered her head into the bottom bunk. My eyes must have reflected that same ember—how she had no problem finding them in the crevice where the mattress met the wall. How she stared long enough that it felt like everything around me darkened and fell away.

~

The tattoo was my idea, had decided on it as I woke. The metallic buzz of the gun called me into the living room. Andy sat at the dining room table drawing roses on an unripe banana. She had her contacts out, and I'd forgotten how bulky her glasses were— the tortoise shell squares obscuring her cheekbones. The moment before she saw me, when I was just standing in my underwear and shirt watching her alone with her art, is a pure sort of memory, a vessel unchanged by time, something never recolored or recast when I reflect on the night before. Just Andy, her bare foot on the circular pedal, a look of concern for her every line. I said, "You should give me a tattoo. I'd pay."

She said, "Put your pants on."

I told her I was serious, and when I donned my jeans and sat down next to her, she said she hadn't worked with skin yet. I said I'd be her first. She was worried about not having stencils to over- lay the image, and I told her to free hand it. A bowl of fruit at the center of the table held granny smith apples, oranges, three bananas dangling like fingers over its lip. I gestured at it, asked if she minded, and she shook her head. Over the tang of the apple, I told her I wasn't nervous. I held up an orange she'd drawn teeth onto, said, "Your lines are great."

She closed off the last petal on the rose, held the banana into the slanting light coming through the window. "What do you want?"

I said something simple. About the size of a baseball. Her design. Palming an orange from the bowl, she dabbed the needle into the ink and stepped on the pedal. I posted my hand on the back of her chair, leaning in to watch her draw. The line curved a half circle, drops of black running down the rind. Andy set the gun down, turned in her seat, said, "Buy me breakfast."

When she rotated toward me, our faces shared a brief and inti- mate space. We worked forty hours arm-to-arm, reaching over each other to grab cups, to trash grounds, bending at the waist to get milk from the fridge below our station, yet this nearness startled me. Green eyes ringed with red, a strand of bangs stuck under her glasses, that string of freckles on the bridge of her nose. The muscles in my face twitched against stillness. I didn't want to be the first one to turn away, but her resolve filled me with a feebleness like hunger. I gathered my shoes and wallet, said I'd be back, forgot to ask her what she wanted to eat.

The air in Charles Village was that dense sort of cold, not quite damp but cool enough to confuse your skin. I could feel the impending rain even before I saw the dark clouds lingering over the tenements. On breaks at work, we'd often split cheap breakfast sandwiches, figured she'd be okay with that, so I went to the Uni Mart up near Hopkins. On the walk back, under the boughs of half-bare trees, the pulse of traffic whipping south on St. Paul, I almost forgot that I lived twenty minutes north, catty-corner to a Dairy Queen in an apartment with its windows painted shut.

She said, "This is how it's going to work—you're not allowed to see it until it's done."

I set the paper bag on the table, handed her one of the styrofoam cups of shitty coffee, asked if she was going to draw a penis on me. She said, "Not just a penis. Balls, too."

While we ate, we decided where it would sit on my body. I wanted it on my arm, blended with my older work, but she said it had to be out of view in case it came out awful. She needed skin that was easy to work with, to start slow. We settled on my right shoulder, just before the blade turned the corner of my outer arm. I took off my shirt, sat backwards in my chair while she washed her hands. Snapping on latex gloves, she set a soda lid upside down on a paper towel, filled it with ink. The cool air ridged my skin with goosebumps, and I put my forearms on the backrest, felt suddenly aware of how my stomach naturally distended in this position. The scrape of the pedal as she repositioned the wire, the gun, settling in the chair behind me. She thumbed Vaseline onto the paper towel, cleared her throat.

"Are you worried?" she said, placing her gloved hands on my shoulders, and I could still feel her warmth through the rubber, and in it, my willingness. Told her I was ready, and she said, "Okay, cause I'm worried."

I said, "What's the worst that could happen?"

For a few minutes, she just pulled on the flesh over my shoulder blade, said she was jealous of how tan I was, how little body hair I had. As the needle bit into my skin, I concentrated on how full I was from breakfast. A tattoo, here, didn't hurt enough to cause distress, just enough pain not to go ignored, but ten minutes in, I was numb to it. That's what no one ever told me, that what makes an easy tattoo is whether the skin goes numb, if it deadens at all. I asked her how it was looking, and she said she was just finishing up the pubic hair. She took a breath, wiped away the excess ink, the blood, said, "You'll see when I'm done."

Time moves so strangely when you're getting tattooed—the constant state of minor shock bending the length of your thoughts. I wasn't worried that she might put some ugliness in me, that I wouldn't like it. What lurched in me—what I held onto—was that willingness, hoping she could see it, that it might salvage me. Last night had been a misstep, but look at how I'm righting the way. Her foot came off the pedal, the wet paper towel cleared the skin, some more Vaseline. She said, "I didn't know you liked Carmen."

I tilted my head toward her and she used her free hand to push my face away from the tattoo. I said, "I didn't either."

Andy said Carmen had a habit of getting involved with her friends. I remember blaming it on the booze, wasn't in my right mind, that the temptation was stronger than I am, and she said sometimes strength is in what you don't do. I didn't hear her, then, not the words, but the meaning—the rattle of the gun's motor vibrating, the drops of blood leaving me one by one. When it was finished, she rubbed it clean, bandaged it with paper towels, pinned them down with the blue painter's tape. I protested, wanted to see before she sealed it, but I never knew how to argue with her, how to get my way.

We grabbed a cab south, picked her car up from Sonar's lot, hopped on 83 toward Towson. I asked her how she felt now that she had her first one finished, and she said, "It's good to know it's done."

The day slipped away from me. Alone in my apartment, I rushed to the bathroom and peeled back the bandage. You're supposed to pool warm water over the wound until the roughed skin feels like skin again. I sat on the edge of the tub, made of bowl of my left hand and lifted the water to my shoulder, wiping carefully. The hurt of the cleaning rivals the work itself, the water agonizing the wound. When my palm caught the skin ridged with ink free, now, of Vaseline, I stood and dried my hands. Fall air traipsed through my apartment's thin walls, put a shiver in me. Had to twist my body in the mirror to see the breadth of it, and I realized I would never know it as she saw it, looking down over my nape.

The next couple of years, we spent some of our Fridays in Sonar, dancing out the week. Carmen never got bored enough to give me her attention again, but I was trying to raise myself to a place where Andy might forgive my misstep. Eventually, change set upon us in that unseen way that flowers never bloom when you're looking, or if you are, the slowness to the opening goes unnoticed. When their lease ended, they moved into a two-bedroom in Towson, closer to me but farther from the things we liked to do together. Then Andy's schedule got switched, and I moved for school. I could almost forget that life, until, in a reflection, I catch a glimpse of the tattoo as I removed my shirt, or a woman's hands run across my naked shoulder, asking me to explain it.

What she'd drawn was black ink on my russet skin, thin lines and stippled shading—the dots collecting in every angle to add depth. It healed well, no scabs catching too roughly the inside of my shirt and pulling free the ink, and while it isn't as bold as my other pieces, there is a certain gentleness about it unique to my body. It was a fist. Finger-side out, delicate nail beds, her hand closed around something unseen. The more I search it, the simpler it is to see that the fist is not grasping, not fighting to hold in its contents. The looseness of the fingers could be pulled back if pried, and yet they are in stone, permanently bridled. There's no shortcut to defining it—there is no single word to capture, fully, its memory. Each word leads to another. And another. And this.

Acknowledgments

I'd like to thank the editors and journals that believed in these stories. "Heaven for Your Full Lungs" originally appears in *American Short Fiction*, whose editorial staff is truly incredible. "Hung Do's Kung Fu" was the runner-up for the Wabash Prize in Fiction and appears in *Sycamore Review*, judged by Charles Baxter. "Clean for Him the Ashes" won the fiction prize from *New Ohio Review*, judged by Colm Tóibín. "Brotherhood" won the *Press53* flash prize judged by Jeffrey Condran. "I Want to Be This to Your That" appears in *Barely South Review*. "Fontanelle" was published in the *Belmont Story Review*. "Donut Man" is online at *AGNI*. "Once You've Gone Back Home" was published in *Hot Metal Bridge*. "Gramps" was published in the final issue of *NANO Fiction*. "Mongolian House" appears in *The Spectacle*.

I was never a person who was in love with writing. I wrote because I felt trapped, wanting to create but having no outlet. In that way, I never believed that my stories were worth reading. Without my friends encouraging me to work, I'd never have accomplished this. Sean, Eera, Kalynn—thank you for giving me the confidence to keep at it, even when what I was sending you was hot garbage.

I'd like to thank my mentor, Michelle Herman, for helping me chase the work I wanted to do. Thank you for being a true believer in the value of narrative, and teaching me what that means. I'd like to thank Lee Martin and his resounding love of the written word. Thank you for teaching with kindness, for showing your students that real criticism comes from a place of love and growth rather than venom.

I write because I don't want to feel alone. In the pursuit of it—whatever *it* really is—I've met so many kind and inspiring people. Writing brought me to Ohio. It introduced me to my brother, Terrance Wedin. It never felt as good as stomping our boots on the bar mats, pouring liquor, and counting cash until the sun came up. Who could ever do it better than us?

Photo: Margaret Cipriano

David E. Yee is a bartender in Columbus, Ohio.
He grew up in Maryland.